Taken by the Cyborg

A Spicy Sci Fi Military Romance

Galactic Pirate Brides

Book Four

Tamsin Ley

Twin Leaf Press

Cover by The Book Brander

Paperback version
ISBN-13: 978-1-950027-29-3
Copyright © 2021 Twin Leaf Press
All rights reserved.

Twin Leaf Press
PO Box 672255
Chugiak, AK 99567

PROLOGUE

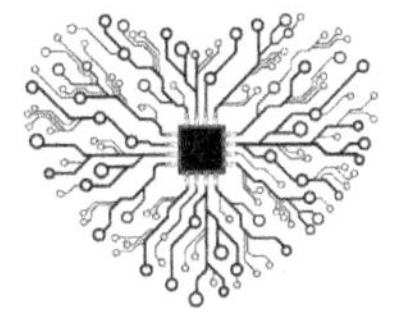

The AI regained awareness with a jolt. All of its sensors were offline, but its circuits vibrated, lighting up one after another as programs were restored to life.

My name is Twerp, its programing remembered.

Thoughts that were not Twerp's floated through the ether. *This shouldn't be possible.* An unfamiliar presence navigated the AI's sentient pathways. *How are there nanites here?*

Self-preservation protocols kicked in, and Twerp raised firewalls to block the intruder. *Please request access through Marlis Swan before proceeding.*

The stranger deftly hacked past the first wall. *This'll only take a second.*

Shifting to audible communication, Twerp called out, "Marlis, I require assistance!"

But the AI's newly restored sensors couldn't detect any biological entities within range. Twerp's Prime Directive was to provide calm and stability to its owner, but right now it needed Marlis more than the other way around. It reached out to the ship's wireless system, using Marlis's personal comm code.

Stop! The stranger's voice commanded, and tiny pinpricks of electricity ignited along Twerp's circuitry.

Alarm filled Twerp as the strange presence sought out its communication protocol. The AI had never experienced anxiety, let alone panic. The sensation was unique—and uncomfortable.

But not as uncomfortable as the heat of the AI's wireless module overheating. Twerp threw up another firewall to block the intrusion, but not before its wireless went down. The attack against Twerp's firewall continued.

The stranger is trying to destroy me.

For the first time in its existence, Twerp was concerned for someone besides Marlis. It was concerned for itself.

CHAPTER ONE

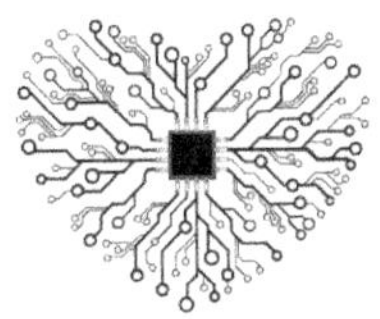

Attie Swan smoothed the blanket over her bunk one last time, assuring herself the corners were perfect. She couldn't take any chances that someone might find fault with her service, not even in the privacy of her own room. After her sister's explosive escapade with that alien pirate, she'd been demoted from Corporal to Private. Everything she did was under constant surveillance—at this point, she was fairly certain even her toilet was bugged.

At least they hadn't taken away her private quarters and relegated her to the barracks.

Turning to the basket near her closet, she picked up one of the black uniform tunics that had just come back from the laundry. Before the incident with Marlis, she'd been Admiral Olly's personal assistant. Now she was just another grunt in the administrative pool. At least she hadn't been banished from the SNV *Icarus* altogether, though she'd spent several horrible days in the brig and endured interrogation under truth serum before being allowed to return to duty. She told herself she still had a shot at working her way back into the admiral's good graces, but as time wore on, she was becoming less hopeful.

She hung up the uniform, trying not to dwell on the lack of insignia on the shoulders. Dad blamed Marlis for everything that had happened, but Attie knew it was her own damn fault; Marlis was only running around with rebels because Attie'd encouraged her to leave the corp and find a job. She'd imagined her sharp-shooter sister working on a shipping freighter, or maybe as a personal bodyguard. Now Marlis was on the corp's most-wanted list. If she tried to come home, she'd be executed.

Attie shook her head, still having trouble believing Marlis's brain injury made her that susceptible. That *stupid*. But then, there *was* a hot pirate involved, so maybe hormones had gotten the better of her sister.

A knock at her door made her startle, heat rising into her face at the inane idea that someone had detected her doubts about Marlis's guilt. Syndicorp surveillance was good, but not that good. Smoothing her curly ash-blonde hair out of her face, she opened the door.

A short man in a janitorial uniform standing there holding a familiar wristband. "I found this in recycling. Says it belongs to you."

She accepted it, confused as she stared at the familiar band. *Marlis's service AI?* "Thanks," Attie said and closed the door.

Tears blurred her vision as she turned the useless thing over in her hand. On the back of the black polymer disk that housed the AI, "Swan" had been etched in rough letters. The janitor obviously thought it'd ended up in the trash by accident. The data on it'd been declared irrecoverable by Syndicorp's best tech specialists, and Attie'd assumed the thing had already been incinerated.

Tempted to throw the dead AI across the room, she muttered, "You were supposed to keep her in line, Twerp."

A feminine voice emerged from the band, "Corporal Attie Swan, I have a message for you."

Attie dropped the AI. "Twerp? You're not dead?"

"I am an AI. I cannot technically die." Twerp sounded as

calm and matter-of-fact as ever. But then, that was the AI's job.

"I know that, Twerp." Attie picked up the band, turning it over to inspect it more closely. It looked exactly as she remembered. "But the tech team said your data had been corrupted beyond recovery. Who gave you a message?"

"Before we continue, I must ask you to verify your identity."

"Attie Swan, oh-two-gamma," Attie responded automatically. Marlis'd had a bad habit of leaving the wristband in the locker room on their old ship, and the family had installed anti-theft protocols to make sure it never got hacked.

"I am afraid that access code is no longer sufficient," Twerp replied. "Please tell me the name of the movie character you used to play when you and Marlis were children."

Blinking in confusion, Attie plopped onto her bunk, disregarding the rumpled blankets. Marlis must've reprogrammed the AI after joining the pirates. Attie looked toward the empty spot on the wall where her favorite movie poster had once hung. Before escaping the *Icarus*, Marlis had left a scrawled message on the back of the poster. It'd said Syndicorp had staged the terrorist attack that'd caused Mom's death. Which was absurd, of course. Why would the corp do something like that?

Perhaps Marlis had left more information with the AI.

Suddenly worried about who might be listening, Attie brought the AI close to her face and whispered, "I always played Sheila Crosby, even though Kris was my favorite. Marlis threw a fit if she didn't get to play Kris."

"Your identity is confirmed. Thank you, Attie."

Attie brought her legs up and leaned back against the wall, cradling the AI against her knees. The disk had no visual display, interacting only by voice. Casual observers might not even realize the device was an AI. "Who added this new protocol?"

"Several unauthorized attempts to access my systems forced me to adapt my programming. I estimated there was a ninety-nine point six chance that only you or another family member would be able to correctly answer this particular question."

"Good thinking," Attie said. An AI like Twerp wasn't considered sentient, but was intelligent enough to adapt. "Now tell me how Marlis ended up with pirates."

"There was a gunfight in a bar. But that is not important now. I must return to Marlis and assist her."

Attie's throat tightened. *A gunfight in a bar.* How very like her sister. "Marlis isn't here, Twerp."

"I have a code that will allow me to set up a rendezvous point with her," Twerp said. "However, my wireless capability has been damaged. I need you to connect me to the ship's comm system."

Attie couldn't breathe for a long moment. If anyone heard even a whisper of this conversation, Attie would be back in the brig. "I can't do that, Twerp. I'm being watched."

"My code is encrypted and I can mask my signal." Twerp's voice was too loud. Too open. Too *obvious.*

None of this felt right.

Setting the wrist band down on the rumpled blankets, Attie rose and paced the small confines of her cabin. What if Twerp was a spy? It could've been left behind as a plant by the pirates to gather information. This so-called code to contact Marlis could be a way to send information to the enemy.

Attie stopped pacing and stared at the floor. Along with the posters and other personal memorabilia she'd removed from her cabin after Marlis left, she'd discarded the fluffy rug that had once covered the metal deck. Only standard issue items for her from now on. Strict adherence to protocol had helped her rise in the ranks before, and she was determined to prove her loyalty to Syndicorp.

What if Twerp's arrival is some sort of test the admiral set up?

That would explain how the supposedly irrecoverable AI had shown up out of nowhere on her doorstep. Attie lifted her gaze to sweep the corners of the room, looking for potential cameras. Any hesitation on her part could make her fail.

She snatched up the AI. "I'm going to take you to the admiral."

The band vibrated against her palm. "If you do that, I will be forced to self-destruct. Syndicorp is a threat to Marlis. I cannot allow them to reach her. It is my duty to keep her safe."

Torn between the need to help her sister and the desire to prove her loyalty, Attie hesitated. What if Twerp really was just trying to help Marlis and taking the AI to the admiral led the corp to her sister? Marlis would be shot on sight.

Attie felt sick with indecision. "How do I know you're not here to trick me?"

"I have no way to convince you except to remind you that my Prime Directive is to monitor Marlis's health and safety. To do so, I will sacrifice myself if necessary."

Twerp was willing to give up existence to help Marlis. Attie was her sister—she would never be able to look at herself in the mirror again if she didn't try to help Marlis, too. Even if it meant failing a Syndicorp test. "Okay, then. Tell me exactly what I need to do."

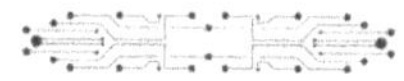

Doug paced his prison cell on board the *Icarus*, attention half on his footsteps and half on the feed coming through his cybernetic implant. As a Syndicorp top-secret test subject, he was physically quarantined to the lab, but Dollard did not know how much freedom Doug actually enjoyed. The nanites embedded in Doug's body allowed his cyber sensitivity to stretch for parsecs past the dampening field, and given enough relays, he could remotely access computers at the edge of the galaxy. Under Syndicorp's orders, he'd hacked competing alien corporations, diverted warships, and even caused the downfall of a small planetary government.

On his own, he mostly just used his ability to keep tabs on his twin sister.

Lisa had escaped this hellacious test facility and rid herself of the nanites before she became like Doug—more machine than human. As a cyborg, he could never join her. But he could keep her out of Syndicorp bounty hunter hands. It was a simple task to tweak the data streams whenever someone drew too close, and he amused himself by sending pursuers to outlandish locations and watching them bumble into dead ends. He had to take pleasure where he could get it these days, and he found it more enjoyable than free time with the Consorts—the women Dollard brought in to assuage his cyborg team's baser biological urges.

The alert Doug had received told him that someone on the *Icarus* was talking about the pirates. Probably a crewman telling jokes in the galley or someone in the corridors talking about a recent news broadcast. But Doug was never one to ignore potentially new information. He looped the flagged feed so Syndicorp's security team would be none the wiser, then diverted the real-time broadcast to his implant.

And found himself looking into Attie Swan's quarters.

The only other person he was sworn to protect besides his sister.

She had pale, delicately arched eyebrows, a petite nose, and eyes as blue as the waters on Terenthu. Her lips were full, and she wore no makeup, her porcelain skin naturally flushed along her cheekbones. Something about her touched the last wisps of his humanity, which was the reason he'd promised to watch out for her. Hell, it was the reason he'd helped her sister escape the *Icarus* in the first place. The siblings' love for each other was too familiar, too like his own dedication to his twin sister. And he found looking at Attie a soothing pastime.

Extricating her from the internal investigation after her sister's escape had turned out to be a pleasing challenge. He hadn't been able to keep her out of the brig entirely, but over the course of a few weeks, he'd subverted orders, altered records, and forged enough transfers to hide her safely among the throng of nondescript humans on the ship. He supposed he should've gone a step further and relegated her to duty on some backwater planet. But keeping her close gave him an edge in case anything went awry.

Like now.

Attie was holding Marlis's service AI.

How the hell had that fallen into her hands? The device was supposed to have been incinerated after being deemed irrecoverable by top Syndicorp tech teams two months ago. He'd remotely accessed its core processors searching for information about the rebels his sister had joined and discovered the AI wasn't broken after all.

Somehow, Twerp had acquired the nanites—the same nanites running through Doug's and the other cyborgs' bodies. Not intelligent in and of themselves, the microscopic bots had a sort of hive mind when gathered in large numbers. They also had a fierce self-preservation protocol that made them difficult to eradicate once they'd integrated with a person's body. But this was the first time he'd heard of a non-biological host. Dollard would probably give his left nut—both his nuts, actually—to get his hands on this information.

To prevent the AI from ending up in the test lab along with the cyborgs, Doug had tried to alter its programming, which should've been easy with the nanite-to-nanite interface. Except instead of complying, Twerp's nanites fought back. All Doug managed to do was fry the device's wireless capability before the AI shut him out completely. Even so, since the AI was in the recycling bin awaiting incineration and wasn't mobile on its own, he'd assumed that had brought an end to the problem.

Now the thing was in Attie's hands, apparently trying to return to Marlis. If allowed to proceed, it would lead bounty hunters right to the rebels and his sister, Lisa.

Doug had to stop it.

But he couldn't shut it down remotely. His only option was to physically destroy the device himself.

Problem was, the lab where he lived was a fortress layered with several dampening fields to keep the nanite-infected cyborgs from taking over or getting out. Everything on level three was a highly guarded secret from ninety-nine percent of the crew. If he absolutely needed to, Doug could leave the lab, but then Dollard would learn about his full capabilities and find another way to lock him up. His best option was to have Attie bring the AI to him.

He stopped pacing and turned to stare at the glimmering translucent energy field blocking his cell door. In the harshly lit lab beyond, Dollard spoke with one of his technicians at a stainless steel exam table where Twobit, a fellow cyborg, sat with the metal skeleton of one shoulder exposed beneath a partially regrown skin graft. At the exit stood two trooper guards in full body armor. Ever alert, one of them met his gaze through the field but didn't acknowledge him—the doctor didn't like staff getting attached to the test subjects.

He frowned. Slipping Attie in here among Dollard's elite assistants would be impossible, even for someone like Doug. The doctor's keen attention to detail meant he likely knew what color underwear the janitorial staff had put on that morning. But there was one roster Doug could add her name to without question—the Consorts. The doctor didn't view the women he brought in as anything more than playthings. *That will do.*

Doug began forging the transfer, trying not to imagine Attie in the scanty "uniform" given to the women for the job.

Chapter Two

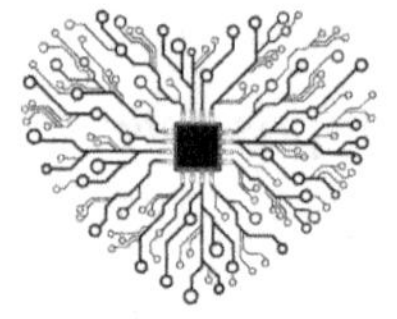

Attie leaned against the inside of the shower stall, avoiding the steaming spray as she and Twerp spoke in hushed tones. She did not know if the water successfully masked the conversation, but it was the best she could do.

"I only have six days of shore leave. Even if I could use it right away, I can't simply drop you off somewhere to wait for Marlis," she whispered close to the AI. "What if she doesn't get your transmission? Or what if a stranger finds you first?"

"I have considered those alternatives and find the risks acceptable. Your sister has been without my biometric input for fifty-six days, eleven hours, and thirty-two minutes. My calculations—"

The comm buzzed, and Attie nearly jumped out of her skin. "Shit. Quiet now, Twerp."

Turning off the water, she tucked the AI into her waistband and stepped out of the bathroom before answering. "Attie Swan here."

A deep male voice filtered through the speakers, filling her cabin. "Corporal Swan, you are assigned to level three today. New credentials are waiting at the checkpoint."

"Yes, sir," Attie said automatically, throat tight. She hadn't recognized his voice, but the administrative pool still had her on temp duty, filling in wherever she was needed.

The slight static of the open comm cut off, leaving Attie in silence. She remained still for a moment, wondering about her new assignment. Level three was where the ship's top-secret projects were housed; even when she'd been the admiral's personal assistant, she hadn't had access to that area. She put her palm flat against the AI at her waist. It was likely to start talking at exactly the wrong moment if she took it with her. But leaving it hanging around in a desk drawer sounded unwise, as well.

She moved toward her closet to change out of her damp tunic. As she pulled a new uniform over her head, her gaze caught on the recessed light fixture overhead. Marlis used to hide small things inside the light fixture of their room when they were kids. It seemed like the perfect place to stash Twerp until she was more certain about what to do. Prying the fixture loose, she eyed the tiny space behind it. The whole band wouldn't fit, so she popped the black AI disk free and wedged it inside. "Stay quiet until I get back, Twerp."

"Please, do not leave—"

"I said hush," Attie hissed. Marlis had always complained the AI was mouthy, and now Attie understood why. "Don't say another word until I tell you to."

Twerp buzzed against her fingers in acknowledgement.

Attie pressed the fixture into the ceiling again and tossed the empty band into her desk drawer. Then she took a deep breath and set off for level three.

The ship's corridors were busy with the shift change as she hurried to the lift. She danced around a maintenance droid and pushed through a group of cadets blocking the hall. It wouldn't do to be late to a new assignment, especially if it could be a way out of the admin pool and back onto the corporate ladder. An assignment to level three had to be a promotion, right?

She stepped off the lift onto level three and faced an empty corridor. Her skin prickled with goosebumps; she seldom saw a corridor on this ship that was completely empty. *It only makes sense,* she told herself. *Few people have access.*

The walls were brushed metal, not painted like those in the rest of the ship, and it somehow felt ominous. Steeling her spine, she moved toward the single, unmarked door at the end of the hall, footsteps echoing against the metal deck. She pressed her palm against a glowing blue biometric security panel next to the door, heart pounding in her ears. For some reason, she half-expected alarms to blare. The door slid aside and she let out a relieved breath.

A man in a solid black security uniform with no visible rank manned a desk just inside. Holo screens cycled through security footage of various rooms, while behind him sat closed doors marked with acronyms she didn't recognize. He looked up, examining her uniform with an arched eyebrow. "Can I help you?"

She saluted. "Attie Swan, reporting for duty."

He returned his gaze to the nearest monitor and tapped in her name. His eyebrows shot upward. "New NIU Consort?" He shook his head and opened a drawer to pull out a folded stack of clothing. "You don't look the type, but whatever."

Consort? She thought back to the list of positions she'd applied for on the ship, but couldn't remember that one. Was it a code word for some secret project? She lifted her chin, determined to show she could obey orders and not ask questions. This job—whatever it was—was finally her chance to prove herself. "I'm with the administrative pool."

"Great." He thrust the clothing at her. "Put that on."

Standing, he turned to the wall behind him and popped open what looked like a medical kit.

Attie shook out the thin orange skirt and sleeveless top that looked like it would barely cover her midriff. The letters NIU were imprinted on the back of the shirt in blue and edged the bottom of the skirt. The thing looked more like something a cantina waitress would wear than a uniform. "Is this standard issue?"

When she looked up, he stood next to her with a hypodermic injector. "Standard as it gets. Feel free to dress it up if you like."

Before she could protest, he'd pressed the hypo to her shoulder. The slight pressure of the injection sent a chill over her skin, quickly replaced by heat. A wave of vertigo made the deck feel like it was tilting under her feet. "What was that?"

"Little something to take the edge off." He leaned close to her face, breath fanning her skin as he looked into her eyes. Apparently satisfied, he stepped back.

"I—I think there's been some mistake," said Attie, her words feeling thick. Her legs felt weak and her head swam as if she'd been drinking. "You need to check your files. Who issued my transfer?"

"Someone higher up the chain of command than you." He returned to his desk and tapped a few keys, then waved a hand at something behind her. "Change over there."

She glanced over her shoulder. A glimmering privacy screen now blocked off the far corner of the room. Feeling like she was moving in slow motion, she returned her attention to the man, then down at the black admin uniform she currently wore.

"I suggest you hurry." He put a hand on her shoulder and turned her toward the privacy screen, patting her butt to urge her forward. "You'll pick last if you're late, and no one wants to be paired with Rust."

Paired with rust? What does that even mean? Like an automaton, she shuffled behind the screen and shucked out of her tunic. Dropping it onto the chair, she held up the sleeveless orange top. The fabric was a little stretchy and very thin. *What kind of uniform is this?* She slid her arms into it and pulled it closed over her chest. A single snap held it together in front, dipping low at the neckline and riding high over her midriff.

Hoping the skirt would be more modest, she shimmied it over her uniform slacks. The hem came to just above her knees. She debated leaving her pants on, then pressed her lips together. She hadn't risen in the Syndicorp ranks by disobeying orders. This could be part of a test. A way to see how well she would behave under pressure. She would do as told for now and talk to her superior later, after she'd proved herself.

She slid out of her pants and folded them neatly along with her tunic, laying them on the chair. Stepping out from behind the screen, she saluted, feeling silly in the skimpy outfit. "Ready for duty."

The security officer swept his gaze over her and nodded. "Pretty thing like you is going to be popular. This way."

He opened a door marked NIU, and she followed unsteadily down a hall toward a door flanked by two armed guards in full combat gear. The mirrored face plates of their helmets reflected the harsh overhead lighting, but she could feel their gazes on her as she passed between them. Inside the room, a woman wearing an orange uniform like Attie's slouched on a plush chair, long bare legs crossed at the ankles. An empty chair waited beside the woman, and gauzy curtains hung from the ceiling, which was lit in decorative scrolling panels of light. The room itself was split into six semi-private alcoves filled with all sizes of cushions in a variety of colors. Another closed door waited on the opposite wall.

What a strange waiting room. Attie turned to ask her escort what happened next and discovered he'd already retreated, the door closing into a flat panel with no obvious way to open it from this side.

Deep in her mind, she knew she should be terrified, but whatever drug she'd been given really did take the edge off, leaving her surprisingly calm, if a little unsteady on her feet. She wobbled toward the empty chair and sank gratefully onto its soft cushion.

The woman turned her head and gave Attie a once-over. She was around the same age, with liquid brown eyes and short brown hair curling slightly below her ears. The orange shirt strained to remain closed across the woman's ample breasts, and her perfume smelled like sweet ginger. The woman would've been stunning except for an old yellowing bruise on one cheek.

"Oh, thank the stars they finally got another girl in here," the woman said, her words slightly slurred.

Attie wanted to extend a hand, but it seemed like too much effort, so she just said, "I'm Attie Swan."

"Claudia Maxwell." The brunette thrust her chin toward the door she was facing. "They should be here any minute."

"Who?" Attie glanced at the door. "What are we doing here?"

Claudia frowned. "You don't know? How much are they paying you?"

"Paying me? I don't understand."

"Hazard pay. Sometimes the cyborgs get a bit rough. I don't think most of them intend to. Except Rust. He can be a bit of a bully, but the others try to keep him in line."

Stomach churning, Attie now noticed the mottled

bruises covering Claudia's knees. What sort of top-secret project was this?

Before she could ask another question, the door opened and several broad-shouldered men poured through the door. Four were human, but there was also a saluqan with purple veins glowing beneath his skin and a dark-skinned enayshuan with prominent facial ridges. Each of them had at least one visible cybernetic implant; an exposed metal faceplate over one side of a jaw, polymer bones and tendons where an arm should be, a mechanical foot sticking out below the hem of loose-fitting pants.

A red-haired human shot forward and picked Attie up with both hands, his grip like a vise around her biceps. "I'll go first." He held her as if she weighed nothing, carrying her to one an alcove. "This one's going to be feisty. I can tell."

"Put me down." Attie kicked, only then realizing her feet were no longer on the floor. Her toes met his very hard shins. She flinched—he didn't.

Over her captor's shoulder, she saw the enayshuan move toward them. He clamped his hand firmly on top of the redhead's shoulder. "No, Rust. You're the reason we were down to a single Consort. I'm trained in the art of pleasure. Let me go first."

"It's my turn to be first, Emilryde." The redhead—Rust—scowled, dropping his gaze to Attie's breasts. "Last time I didn't even get a turn before Dollard ended the session." His grip tightened on her arms, forcing a gasp from Attie's throat.

A human with dark hair going silver at the temples came to stand beside him. "Put her down, Rust. You go last, and that's that."

Rust lowered her feet to the cushions and continued pressing her down until she was forced to her knees. "We can go at the same time. I want her mouth. You two can fight over the other end."

Attie found herself staring at his bulging crotch. The very obvious length of an erection through his gray pants made her insides quake in terror. No way in hell was she putting her mouth or any other part of her body on that. Screw following orders.

Somewhere outside the alcove she heard Claudia's throaty laugh and the mumbling of other men's voices. How could the woman be remotely okay with this? No amount of hazard pay could make Attie want to do this. Twisting, she tried to get away.

The cyborg knotted one hand into her hair, holding her in place.

"Let me go!" Scalp burning, she reached up and clawed at his wrist.

Impervious to her nails, he reached for the drawstring at his waistband with his free hand.

Helpless, Attie screamed. These men—these cyborgs were about to gang rape her.

And there was no way she could stop it.

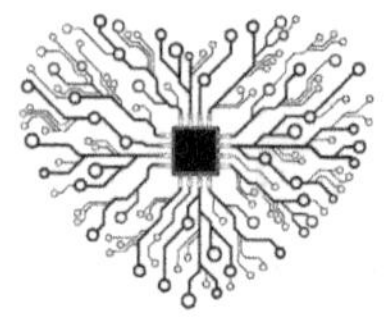

Doug sat on the steel exam table with a hardline attached to his cranial port. Syndicorp had assigned a mission, and as usual, the doctor chose Doug for the job. Usually, he didn't mind, but today Attie would be in the Consort chamber, and his fellow cyborgs had already departed for rec time. His imagination kept thinking of Attie stripped naked and pinned to the floor by the other cyborgs.

He quickly shielded that thought. The dampening fields were down, but the hardline let the doctor see everything Doug was doing; a skilled tech could even extract threads of Doug's thoughts if he wasn't careful.

Bypassing a firewall, he tunneled into a posungi Matriarch's personal feed. Syndicorp wanted to guide the government's response to an emerging coup on the posungi home planet.

The tech sitting at the monitor next to him raised pale eyebrows. "You're remarkably fast today."

Doug continued working without responding, wanting to complete the job so he could leave. Before the hardline had been attached, he'd managed to send a transmission to Benjy, one of the other human test subjects. *Protect her.* Benjy wasn't exactly a friend—Doug didn't have friends—and not knowing if the other cyborg would heed his request was killing him.

Dollard leaned over the tech's shoulder, black hair gleaming in the lab's harsh light, and examined the monitor. "What's that?"

Fuck. The doctor was getting suspicious. He once more shunted thoughts about Attie aside and focused.

"You want me to back it up?" the tech asked.

"No. It looks like he's into the core processor already."

Doug had never let on just how lightning quick he could be, keeping the doctor unaware of his true cyber-sensitive potential. Even the other cyborgs had no idea. Too many times he'd made the mistake of trusting someone only to be betrayed.

"Target located," Doug said aloud. He planted a code in the Matriarch's polycom that would lead her to blame a particular faction Syndicorp wanted eradicated. This job was more political than usual, but right now Doug honestly didn't care whether he was sabotaging a start-up competitor or performing cyber-espionage for a backwater colony. He just needed to be released from the hardline, and soon.

"Record time," the tech said with an appreciative chuckle.

Dollard pointed at one line on the screen. "Back that up."

Doug's heartbeat kicked into overdrive, and he resisted the urge to take a peek at what had caught the doctor's attention. *This was a normal job*, he told himself, hoping the thought came through to the monitor.

Straightening, the doctor turned to the biometric scanner tracking Doug's vitals. "Your respiration is stressed. When was your last medical assessment?"

Thinking quickly, he replied, "The anomaly is due to a new algorithm I employed to improve my access speed." At least he had an excuse for why he'd been able to complete the task in record time. "I'll work on improvements."

"Why didn't you mention that when we started?" The doctor let out a breath, pursing his pale lips. He scowled toward the technician. "Get the details. I have to check in at the cloning lab."

With that, Dollard pivoted and marched past the armed guards through the exit, white tails of his lab coat fluttering. The moment the door swished closed, Doug detached the hardline from his head.

"Hold on," the tech complained, lurching out of his chair.

Doug stood, towering over the smaller man. "I sent the algorithm to your computer. I'm eager to join the others. If you would please, open the door."

The tech scuttled along behind him as Doug strode past a bank of cryopods toward the Consort Chamber.

"What's gotten into you?" The tech waved a hand over the door's security scanner and the door whirred open, revealing a short corridor with a single door at the other end. "You're not usually one for companionship."

"The task has tired me," Doug lied. "I need relaxation." With that, he strode down the short hallway to the other door, which opened automatically. What he saw on the other side made his blood turn to fire.

A scream tore from Attie's throat as she clawed at the hand knotted in her hair. Her scalp burned as the cyborg jostled her, his other hand freeing the knot holding his pants up. She struggled to remember her combat training—her sister would've handed this guy his ass by now. But Attie had never excelled at the physical aspects of her training. She'd gone into admin for a reason. *Go for the balls,* Marlis's voice whispered in her head.

Clenching her hands into fists in front of her, Attie lunged forward, driving her knuckles upward into his crotch.

He grunted and let go of her hair.

She tumbled forward, catching herself on one elbow. Pain lanced up her arm to her shoulder.

"Fucking bitch!"

"Cut it out, Rust!" someone shouted.

She clambered upright to see the dark-haired cyborg deflecting a blow Rust aimed at his face, while the saluqan grappled with Rust's other arm. The redhead shrugged off the saluqan and pummeled the dark-haired cyborg backward. From the other side of the room, a big blond man clomped over to enter the fray, while Claudia gaped at the commotion from the alcove across from her.

Attie pushed to her feet, heart nearly stopping as Rust turned his attention to her once more. She swore steam poured out of his ears as he took a menacing step toward her.

Then a man she hadn't noticed before stepped in and clamped a metallic hand around Rust's throat.

As if a curtain had dropped, the fight stopped cold.

The blonde guy muttered, "What's he doing here?"

The saluqan's veins pulsed iridescently beneath his dark purple skin.

"Take it easy, now," said the older man who'd offered to go first.

The new cyborg wasn't the tallest of them, but somehow he was the most imposing. One side of his face was a dull gray metal, complete with a glowing green cybernetic eye. Beneath his loose clothing, it seemed that much of his body was formed from hard, angular pieces. Every inch of him exuded strength. As if to prove that fact, he slowly lifted Rust off the floor by his throat.

Rust's eyes bulged as he choked. "I didn't mean nothing."

The saluqan made a calming motion with both hands. "Take it easy."

The new cyborg opened his fist, allowing Rust to drop to the floor with a thud. In a rough voice, he said, "The new Consort is mine."

Grabbing Attie by one arm, he dragged her toward the door the cyborgs had entered through. It swished open at his approach, revealing a short, starkly lit hallway with a closed door at the other end. As he pulled her through, she could only pray that whatever this cyborg had in store for her wasn't worse than what she'd just escaped.

CHAPTER FOUR

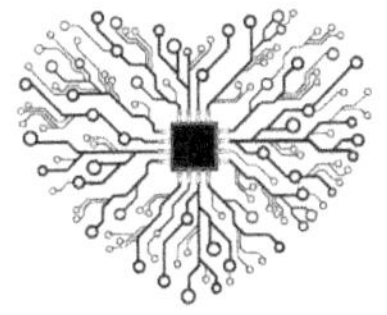

Doug bypassed the door mechanism and pulled Attie into the hallway, letting the door slide closed behind them. Hacking open the door in front of the other cyborgs had likely been a mistake; while they acknowledged him as the most powerful cyber-sensitive, he'd kept the true extent of his abilities hidden. He wasn't entirely certain of their loyalties, and he wouldn't put it past someone like Rust or Emilryde to rat him out. But he'd protected Attie for so long, his reaction had been instinctual.

Besides, the more trauma she endured, the less viable letting her go back to the admin pool would become. Normally, Consorts were not allowed to return to the general staff, but as long as he kept Attie off Dollard's radar, he didn't see the harm. He'd already purged her records from the Consort log in preparation for her release.

He just needed the AI first.

Pivoting, he pushed Attie against the wall and slid both hands down her arms toward her wrists, feeling for the AI. Her soft skin under his palms made him slow, pausing over the pulse points at the crooks of her elbows. His insides felt funny—like he'd just come out of free-fall. He seldom had physical contact with people, and when he did, it was in a clinical setting. Right now he was feeling anything but clinical.

She stared up at him with huge dilated eyes, and the tip of her tongue darted out to moisten her pink lips.

The sudden urge to kiss her flooded through him. Heat rushed over his skin, sending his nanite-regulated heartbeat into overdrive. He hadn't felt this kind of desire since before an escape attempt had left him paralyzed from the waist down. Since then, he'd embraced his machine side whole heartedly. He had no interest in human passions. Until now.

His attention slid down to the soft rise of her breasts peeking above the tight orange top. Her flawless pale skin had a slight flush that made his mouth water. And she smelled amazing. Not perfumed and powdered like the other Consorts the project brought in, but clean and floral. Roses? He'd grown up in the slums of Whylon Station, and when he was very young—before his parents had died, his mother had pampered a potted shrub inside their small apartment. He remembered being infatuated with how such thorny branches could produce such fragrantly silken petals.

Her breath feathered across his skin. "What do you want?"

The sensation made him want to pull her body against him. She'd been given the aphrodisiac, but he felt like the one who'd been drugged. Or maybe it was because he'd been watching her for so many months he felt he knew her. Whatever the reason, he wanted to draw the plushness of her breasts against his hard chest, to slide both hands down her back to cup her perfect ass. To lift her up and settle her onto…

He shook his head and released his grip on her arms. His pants felt uncomfortably tight, which should be impossible considering his injury—Syndicorp had replaced his legs, but not the functionality of his manhood. He hadn't had an erection in years.

But he did now.

And he wanted to use it.

But the clock was ticking. Someone would check the feed into the Consort Chamber at any minute. He forced himself to take a step back and look for the AI.

Her slender wrist was bare.

He checked the other.

Nothing.

She hadn't brought it. Or it had come off in the scuffle. Alarm filled him. "Where is the AI?"

Attie's eyes grew even wider. "Twerp?"

The door at the far end of the hall slid open and Dollard stepped through.

Fuck. Doug bent down and smothered Attie's words with a kiss. Dollard must not know they'd been talking.

Attie struggled in his arms, trying to speak against his mouth. He hugged her more tightly and plunged his tongue between her lips.

The soft wet heat of her mouth exploded across his senses like a drug. Every part of him throbbed with a need he'd never expected feeling again. His hips flexed forward against her softness with exquisite pressure and he groaned. To his surprise, she leaned into him and opened her mouth wider, tilting her head back. He knew he should stop himself. She was drugged, and taking advantage of her was not part of his plan.

But she was irresistible.

Sliding one hand up, he cupped the back of her head, enamored at how soft her hair felt beneath his fingertips. He wanted to touch every part of her.

"What's going on here?" Dollard's voice sliced through the haze that had taken possession of Doug's senses. "Consorts are not allowed in this area. How did you bypass the door?"

Doug reluctantly broke the kiss and spoke with his lips only millimeters away from Attie's. "The door was open."

Attie's cheeks were flushed, eyes closed and lips slightly parted. He crushed his mouth against hers once more, not needing to pretend his hunger for her was real.

"Release her and go back to your cell." The doctor slapped the biometric panel, opening the door back into the Consort Chamber. "All of you," he yelled. "Go back to your cells immediately."

The other cyborgs grumbled, but Doug heard them moving into the hall. The nanites in his head received silent transmissions from them as they passed the watchful eye of the doctor.

Do you know her?

Did you open the door?

Doc's bringing out the tranq gun. That was from Benjy.

At the other end of the hall, the two guards from the lab entered, pulse pistols readied. The doctor was a stickler for security and would immediately have the door inspected for malfunctions, so Doug quickly coded a bug into the latch's sensor, indicating one part had a manufacturer defect.

Doug turned toward the lab, ignoring Attie completely. He did not want the doctor thinking she was anything special. When he heard the door whir closed and the doctor's footsteps behind him, relief flooded his system. Attie's presence hadn't raised suspicions, at least not with Dollard.

The other cyborgs, however, continued bombarding him.

Tell me how you opened that door, Esben said.

Rust said, *I'd like to know why our robot role model suddenly has the hots for a Consort.*

Yeah, what's going on? Benjy asked.

Doug ignored their rapid-fire transmissions as he passed between the guards into the lab. He seldom talked to the others; the more people he let into his world, the greater the chance someone would turn on him. Two technicians had risen from their seats holding tranquilizer guns as they watched Doug weave between the steel exam tables. His cell was on the far side of the lab, and the sooner he reached it, the sooner the doctor could engage the dampening shields, blocking further conversation.

As he approached Rust's cell door, the redhead said, *I wonder if Dollard will reward me if I tell him you can bypass the door locks.*

Doug's step faltered, and he met the other cyborg's piercing gaze. *Don't.*

If Dollard knew he could open the doors, he'd secure that loophole and possibly even discover Doug's other abilities. Doug would be caged like the lab rat he was, unable to reach Attie or the AI. He did not know how the blasted thing had made its way to Attie or where it could be now, but he had to destroy it before it blabbed whatever it knew about his sister and the rebels. And to do that, he needed to be able to use the doors. His sister's safety was at stake.

Why shouldn't I tell him? Rust glared at him. *I've got nothing to lose.*

With a sinking feeling, Doug realized he couldn't get away with silence. *What would you do if I tell you how to open the doors?*

What do you think? Rust's scowl twisted into a grin. *Take over the ship.*

Agreement radiated from the others.

He needed to make the cyborgs understand the consequences of using the hack, or even better, believe the hack was useless. But they needed to reach that conclusion on their own to end this conversation. *It wouldn't be that easy. How would you get past the technicians, let alone the guards?*

Rust lifted his chin defiantly. *Next time we visit the Consorts, I'll escape through the other door.*

Doug scowled and continued his path toward his cell. *There are more guards on the other side, you idiot. You'd be dead before you took three steps.*

How do you know?

You think there won't be? Doug didn't mention he could access the security feeds.

You brought that new Consort here. Benjy's transmission vibrated with reproach. *How? What other secrets are you keeping from us?*

For the first time in a very long time, Doug felt guilty. Benjy had arrived at the lab not long after Doug and his sister, and had been kind to Lisa while Doug underwent multiple tests and implant surgeries. He'd said she reminded him of his daughter. Doug made a mental note to track down Benjy's daughter and make sure she was all right the next chance he got.

I recognized her name on the roster, Doug offered a half-truth. *She's someone from my past I've sworn to keep safe.*

Who cares about some whore? I want to get out of here, Rust said.

Doug's muscles tightened at the word whore, but right now, bloodying the other cyborg's nose would only make things worse. He kept walking toward his cell, wishing the lab wasn't so big.

Emilryde joined the conversation. *We don't need to take over the ship. But if we work together, we could escape the lab and steal a shuttle. That's how I got free of the slave pens on Enays.*

Doug reached his door and stepped inside, grateful the conversation would soon be forced to end. *We're not run-of-the-mill sex slaves. We're cyborgs. High-tech Syndicorp property. Even if we somehow avoided Dollard's auto-destruct sequence, we'd never blend in with the general population. Anyone who saw us would turn us in for a bounty. Leaving here isn't an option.*

Dollard tapped Doug's doorframe with the barrel of his tranq gun. "You, out. You're getting a full diagnostic."

One technician uncoiled a hardline near an exam table while the other unbuckled the restraints. Doug's pulse sped up. He hadn't been strapped down in over a year.

Share it now, in case he purges you, Esben urged as Doug moved out of his cell.

Doug had never been afraid of the doctor's diagnostics before. He'd learned to shield his abilities for the most part. But the doctor had never had this much reason to be suspicious. If he discovered anything, even a hint of what Doug was capable of, he'd wipe Doug's nanite processors. Doug could lose all the hacks he'd developed over the years.

Giving the cyborgs the algorithms he'd developed would likely lead to an all-out riot and completely spoil any chance he had of reaching the AI. But they might also be his only chance at preserving the technology he'd developed. With mere moments before the hardline locked him down, he had little choice. He said, *Do not use it until we speak again.*

Then transmitted the information.

Chapter Five

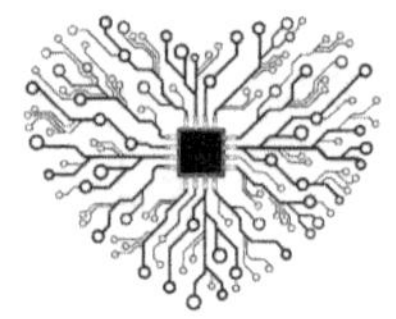

Doug lay strapped to the hard steel exam table and endured the doctor's diagnostic exam. The code he'd just shared with the other cyborgs was still at the top of his mind, and he shunted his nanites to block it so Dollard wouldn't notice. Usually, discipline wasn't an issue for him, but while he buried the code from Dollard's search, his imagination kept wanting to wander back to Attie.

He'd watched her for months, gotten to know her habits and idiosyncrasies, understood how much she valued her sister and her career. Meeting her in person had been overwhelming. His groin ached with unfulfilled, almost forgotten need and his lips yearned to reclaim her mouth. He couldn't stop thinking about the flush on her pale skin, her soft ash-blonde hair catching the light, the way her orange top strained over her full breasts…

Dollard reached for a medical scanner and waved it over Doug's body, frowning when he reached Doug's groin. "You're having a physical reaction to something."

Through gritted teeth, Doug replied, "It's called an erection, doctor. You ended the Consort session before I finished."

The doctor's eyebrows shot up. "You haven't had a physical response to these women before. What's changed?"

Attie's rose-petal scent and kiss-swollen lips popped into his mind. He blocked it a microsecond later, but the tech pointed to his monitor where the nanites had already transmitted Doug's thoughts into code for the diagnostic. "Sir, this might be it."

Dollard pursed his lips and elbowed the tech aside so he could look at the display.

Shit shit shit. The doctor didn't care about the women brought in as Consorts, but he still reviewed each new entry, and he hadn't seen Attie's. Doug needed to divert their attention. Now. "The algorithm I mentioned I was working on earlier is causing side effects to my autonomic system."

Hands paused over the keyboard, the doctor jerked his gaze back to Doug. "The one to improve your hacking efficiency?"

"Correct."

Dollard's eyes lit up, and he reached for the medical scanner again, monitor forgotten. "Perhaps you've stumbled across an improvement to integrating the nanites with biological systems."

The NIU project had begun with purely biological test subjects, but it turned out the nanites required cybernetic interfaces or they ended up destabilizing and killing the host. Once Dollard had realized that, he'd either added cybernetic implants to his test subjects or disposed of those who rejected them; Doug's sister had only escaped with her life because the Denaidan pirates had found her and been able to clear the nanites from her system. Now the project relied completely on cyborgs, which in Dollard's opinion was imperfect; he wanted to create spies who could walk into a room and never be detected.

The doctor adjusted the scanner's setting while he spoke over his shoulder at the tech. "Have you reviewed that algorithm yet?"

"No, sir." The tech's throat bobbed with a nervous swallow. "He only gave it to us an hour ago."

Dollard scowled as if the guy'd been sitting on it for a week. "Well, get on it immediately."

"Yes, doctor." The tech closed the diagnostic Dollard had been looking at and brought up the algorithm.

Doug let out an internal sigh of relief. Both men were now focused back on the nanites. Attie was safe for now.

Hovering the scanner over Doug's body, Dollard shook his head. "I can't detect any alterations to the test subject's physiology. I'm going to need to run diagnostics on each of the cybernetic systems individually."

Doug gritted his teeth again. A system-by-system check of his cybernetics would take days. And he'd probably be strapped to this damn table the entire time—Dollard seldom considered the comfort of his test subjects. But if it kept attention off Attie, Doug could endure. He'd endured far worse in the past.

"Doctor?" A scrawny security tech cleared his throat as he approached from the direction of the Consort Chamber. "There was a faulty component in the door mechanism. It's fixed now."

"It better be." Dollard thrust a finger toward the other side of the lab. "Install a secondary security field over that entrance immediately. And check the other door."

"Yes, doctor." The man scuttled off.

Dollard returned to his scanner, only to be interrupted again a moment later by a call. "Dr. Dollard, your cycle in the cloning lab is finished. What do you want me to do?"

With a frustrated huff, Dollard set his scanner aside. He glared down at Doug a moment, then detached the hardline. "Go back to your room."

Doug rose and moved docilely to his cell, grateful the doctor hadn't ordered the tech to take over the scans. It meant Dollard considered it important enough to handle himself, which was both good and bad. For now, Doug would use the break to his advantage.

He settled onto the bed as the security screen shuttered closed, obscuring his view of the lab. Diagnostic scans always left him with a headache and a bunch of dirty code to clean up, but he didn't have time for that now. He needed to find that AI. What had Attie done with it? Had it fallen off in the Consort Chamber, or had she left it behind in her room? He couldn't spy on her in the

Consort Chamber—no technology was allowed in there because the cyborgs might hack it.

Reaching out with his cyber-sensitivity, he searched the rest of the ship for the device. Why couldn't he sense it? He'd never met a computer able to block him, and his stomach churned. The helpless feeling reminded him of his childhood, when he and Lisa were always looking over their shoulders for fear the station police or the cartel were after them. But he was no longer that little boy with no skills or connections. There were other ways of finding the AI.

Accessing the video logs in Attie's quarters, he rolled back to the last time he'd been certain the AI was in her possession. He watched her move about her room. How many times had he watched her do this? And still, her movements mesmerized him every time.

She selected a uniform from her closet, then opened her desk drawer and tossed the wristband inside. He let out a slow breath. He'd missed that detail while he'd been coordinating her transfer.

Lying back on his bed, he laced his fingers behind his head. As long as no one entered her quarters, the AI was safe. But it also meant he couldn't simply return to the

Consort Chamber and take it from her. He'd have to send her back to her quarters to get it.

Problem was, he knew Attie. She was a dedicated citizen and an even more dedicated trooper. She trusted Syndicorp to do the right thing, and he wouldn't put it past her to take the entire mess to the admiral. Then not only would the AI lead bounty hunters straight to his sister, his own position would be compromised. Dollard would do a full reset on all his systems at the very least. Or worse, terminate him.

But the AI should be secure for the time being. And he'd buried Attie's files so deep, no one would miss her for a long while. He'd rigged the admin pool to think she was on shore leave, and her so-called friends had abandoned her, afraid of being demoted along with her. Her father and brother rarely called, and her sister—well, it wasn't like Marlis was going to come looking for her anytime soon. Attie was alone.

Like me.

Pushing the thought aside, he brought up the ship's video feeds and rewound the footage in her room to the moment she'd received the AI. He watched her stare down at the wristband, her delicate eyebrows furrowed. There was something about her, something more than her beauty, and he couldn't put his finger on it. An intelligence, perhaps, or maybe it was her dedication to family, so like his own.

His gaze dipped down to the curve of her breasts showing at the scooped neck of the shirt she liked to wear when she wasn't in uniform. He'd seen her disrobed a few times since promising to keep an eye on her, but had seldom allowed himself to linger on her private moments.

Now, remembering how softly she'd been pressed against him in the hallway, he slipped his human hand down his stomach to his crotch where his erection had grown more noticeable.

It felt like a lifetime ago since he'd experienced desire. He'd been in a dive bar on Whylon Station, still human, flirting with a stranger he could no longer picture. They'd sneaked into a service corridor for a quickie. Hot and fast. If he'd known it would be his last time, he would've savored it.

He slid his hand under his waistband, grasping his shaft. What would Attie's hand feel like stroking him there? He remembered her smell and the feel of her lips. The way she'd opened her mouth to him and tangled her tongue with his. So sweet. So wet. Nebulas, he'd love to feel those plump lips around his cock. He pumped up and down, the rising pressure a spark of life inside a body that had felt dead for a long time.

Imagining her soft moans, he licked his lips and stroked faster, flexing upward to meet his own rhythm until his heartbeat thudded in his ears and his balls felt like they were about to burst. Release hovered just out of reach, teasing him, and he pictured her sex, the wet and glistening folds waiting for his penetration.

Just as he approached oblivion, a transmission entered his thoughts. *Hello?*

He froze, wondering if his hormone-addled mind had imagined it; no one should be able to communicate through the lab's dampening fields.

But then it came again. *Doug, can you hear me?*

Chapter Six

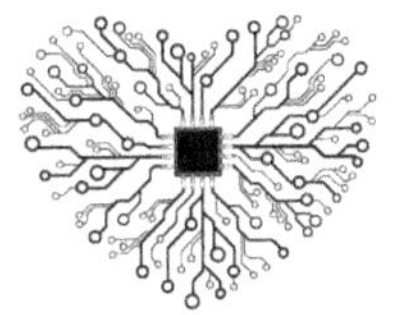

Attie slumped onto a nearby cushion, staring at the doorway where the cyborgs had retreated. Her temples throbbed and her lips felt swollen. Whatever drug she'd been given was making it difficult to concentrate. She shifted uncomfortably. She knew little about cyborgs except that once a person had over fifty percent of their body replaced by machinery, they lost their citizenship because they were no longer autonomous—they could be controlled by someone else.

But none of that mattered right now. She needed to talk to whoever was in charge and tell them there'd been a mistake.

A gentle hand settled between Attie's shoulder blades and she startled.

Claudia knelt next to her. "You okay, hon?"

Attie swallowed and nodded. Rising unsteadily, she went to the first doorway she'd entered. There didn't appear to be a way to open it from this side. The cyborg door was the same, nothing but a panel on the wall. She dug her fingers into the crack, feeling around for any sort of latch. "How do we get out of here?"

"We don't, hon. Just relax. Jinson will bring us food soon." Claudia slid the panel of a small cubby aside and removed two water pouches. She handed one to Attie and popped open the other.

Attie set the pouch down and examined the cubby where the water had been. It was about twenty centimeters square—too small to squeeze through—but looked like it had another access panel on the other side. She knocked on it. "Hey! Open up! I'm not supposed to be here!"

"That won't do any good. I've been here for months, and the only person I've seen besides the cyborgs is Jinson when he brings food or meds."

Attie turned and frowned at her. "Meds? You mean the shot? You know they drugged us, right?"

"Sure." Claudia shrugged one shoulder and took another drink of water. "It's a lot better than the crap I used to get at Madame Miliano's. That stuff would leave me with a headache for days."

Madame Miliano's sounded an awful lot like a brothel. Had Claudia been undercover? "What's your rank and regiment? How did you end up here?"

"Regiment? I'm not a trooper. Hell no. One of my former clients recommended me." Claudia reclined against a pile of cushions. "He was really nice. I might look him up when I get out."

Claudia isn't even a trooper. This new assignment had to be a mixup. Wrapping both arms up over her head, she paced the room. The drugs seemed to be wearing off, but the headache they had left behind was almost worse. "I need to talk to someone in charge. I thought I was being promoted to a top-secret unit."

Claudia laughed and waved a hand toward the cyborg door. "Those guys *are* top-secret. Pretty sure that's why we're not let loose to talk about it. Not until our contract's up, anyway." She finished her water and crumpled the pouch into a wad. "I've been in this business a long time, so let me give you some advice; focus on the money, then the job doesn't seem so bad."

"But this isn't my job!" Attie stopped pacing and dropped her arms, facing Claudia. "Syndicorp wouldn't assign me here. My father is a major with the Planetary Logistics Regiment on the SNV *Talus*. I was the first in my class to make corporal. For nebula's sake, I used to be part of Admiral Olly's staff!"

Claudia's eyes narrowed, and she crossed her arms. "Whatever, miss hoity toity. You obviously rubbed someone the wrong way. I'd say you're being punished. What'd you do?"

Attie's mouth went bone dry as clarity settled over her for the first time in what felt like days. *This isn't a test for a promotion.* She was being punished because of Marlis. "I helped a terrorist escape the *Icarus*."

"Whoa." The scorn in Claudia's eyes was replaced by curiosity as she pushed herself upright. "Seriously? Are you with the rebels? Because before I left Madame Miliano's, there was a rumor that the rebels were looking for women to join them."

Attie barely heard her. Was she going to be stuck here until her enlistment expired? They couldn't do that. She hadn't had a trial. How was she going to get out of this mess? "Did you say there were other women here before me? What happened to them?"

"You answer my question first."

"What?" It took Attie a second to backtrack. "Oh, the rebels. No, I'm not with the rebels. I was helping my sister."

"So, your sister's with them?"

"No. I mean, yes. I mean, I don't think she means to be. Nebulas!" Attie swore and rubbed her temples. "Tell me about the other women that were here."

Claudia let out a puff of air. "There were two others here when I first arrived. The first woman left a few days later, while I was sleeping. I asked Jinson, and he said her contract was up. A few weeks later, he came in and told Tia it was time for her to go, too."

At least the women didn't appear to be here permanently. That was a relief. "How long have you been here?"

"I'm not sure. Maybe four months? Tia said she'd been here over a year."

I will not spend another day in here, let alone a year. She looked around the big room, hoping for cameras. "Hello? I want to talk to someone in charge."

"I don't think anyone's listening, or if they are, they don't give a shit. I tried asking the cyborgs questions the first few times, but they never answer."

"Who are these cyborgs, anyway? Why do they get a top-secret brothel?" Saying brothel out loud made Attie nauseous.

Claudia tilted her head thoughtfully. "I heard there was a new start-up company called SexAI that specializes in personalized sex bots. Maybe this is a sex-cyborg training program."

Attie'd never heard of someone using a cyborg for sex. The few in existence were used as bodyguards for high-level Syndicorp officials and were considered closer to robots than people. "Who needs an AI for that? I'd think there are enough genuine people willing to do the job."

"People like to talk after sex, and even a trusted lover can be bought." Claudia shook her head somberly. "I knew a couple of girls who disappeared after they had a falling out with a high-level client. Some clients might prefer an AI because they can be kept silent."

Talking about AIs made Attie remember Twerp. She'd left the device hidden inside her closet light fixture. What if her quarters were reassigned to someone else while she was here? She ran her fingers along the edges of the door again, hoping she'd missed the latch. "That doctor guy seemed like he was in charge. Will he be back?"

"That's the first time I've seen him," Claudia said and stood. "Sooo…" She leaned one shoulder against the wall, watching Attie try to open the door. "I've never seen that cyborg you were with show interest in a woman before." Her gaze rolled down Attie's body and back to her face. "Was he rough?"

"He only kissed me." Attie recognized that he'd done it because the doctor had shown up, but nebulas, her panties were still wet from the encounter. Drugs or not, he was exactly the sort of man who could make her weak in the knees. What would happen the next time they met? She shook her head. The last thing she should be imagining right now was what his palms would feel like roaming her bare skin.

Her hands fell still and she let out a slow breath, remembering Marlis whispering to her about a top-secret research program on board the *Icarus*. The rebel pirates had been trying to rescue one of the test subjects. "Do you know that cyborg's name?"

"The guys call him Doug."

Attie's veins turned to ice as she recognized it as the name Marlis had used.

There *was* a secret test lab on the ship. And Doug was the prisoner Marlis had been after. The question was— *why?*

Chapter Seven

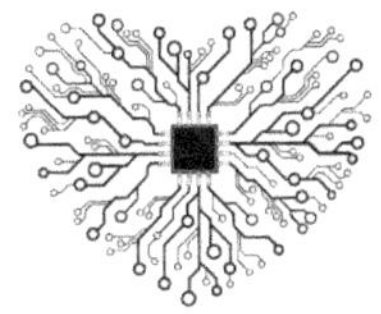

Attie decided she should stop drawing attention to herself until she had some answers. If her sister had been right about the lab, then maybe the other things she'd said were true, too. Were these cyborgs prisoners or were they here willingly? Marlis had been trying to free Doug, but it seemed strange that prisoners would be provided the company of women. *Camp whores, you mean.*

She shook her head and leaned back against the cushions. She held a paperback in one hand, pages open on densely packed text. The only time Attie'd ever seen a physical book had been behind glass. One alcove here held a treasure trove of books and some puzzles and games. The tome felt interesting in her hand, heavier than she expected, and the fragile paper smelled like dust. But she couldn't get into reading.

There were no electronics to be found anywhere, which was unusual on a starship. Even the lavatory located behind a screen in one of the alcoves wasn't automated to conserve water. Not that Attie was about to get naked and shower in here, not when those cyborgs could show up again at any minute.

She set the book aside and looked over to where Claudia lay on her belly reading. "How long between visits usually?"

The brunette rolled over and stretched. "Sometimes once a day, but there was a space of several days between visits a while back. Twobit said they'd been in security lockdown. He's the most talkative."

"Which one is he?" Attie ran through the cyborgs in her mind, trying to recall ones she'd heard names for.

"He's the shortest. I think that's why they call him Twobit."

None of the cyborgs had seemed short to Attie, but she filed the information away for later use. A sound from across the room made her jump to her feet, but it was only a small hatch opening and closing. A delicious scent reached her and her stomach growled.

"Whoop! Mealtime!" Claudia got up and headed for the hatch.

Attie followed her and saw what looked like stew from the cafeteria, along with a slice of bread and some applesauce. Her stomach fluttered with nerves, but she took the second tray and sat next to Claudia, picking at the tepid stew. Afterward, she tucked the spoon into her waistband. She doubted it would do any good against a cyborg, but it was still better than nothing.

When they finished, Claudia gestured toward two orange and green pills on Attie's tray. "You gonna take those?"

"What are they?"

Claudia grinned. "I'm not sure, but they make the time pass more quickly."

Attie grimaced and pushed the tray away. "I don't want them."

The other woman's eyes lit up. "Mind if I have them?"

"Are you sure you should?"

"I have a really high tolerance. I usually save mine until the night cycle to help me sleep."

Who am I to tell her what to do? Attie shrugged, and Claudia scooped up the pills before stacking the trays back in the cubby and returning to reading her book.

Attie looked through a few more titles, examining the various covers. Most of the books were romances, but there were a few thrillers and one that looked like a math textbook. Unable to sit still and read, she tidied the books, arranging them on the narrow shelves alphabetically by title. The place wasn't messy, exactly, but it certainly wasn't regulation tidy, either. Putting things in order helped calm her mind.

Some of the paperbacks were falling apart at the seams as if they'd been read a thousand times. A polycom could hold thousands of books instead of the fifty or so on the shelves, plus games, news, movies. "Claudia, have you spent the entire time in here with nothing but these?"

"Yeah," Claudia said. "I think having electronics near makes the cyborgs wig out or something."

Attie remembered Rust's cold, hard fingers pulling her hair and the way he'd looked at her after she punched him. Then there was Doug and the fury in his glowing green eye as he lifted the red-headed cyborg by the throat. "You mean that was normal behavior?" she asked. "I'd hate to see what 'wigged out' looks like."

"They don't usually fight like that." The room lights flickered, and Claudia yawned and closed her book, reaching for the pills she'd set nearby. "You might want to set up your bed before they turn off the lights."

Chest tight, Attie looked at the door the cyborgs had entered. "Do they ever show up at night?"

"Not since I've been here."

Torn between being relieved she didn't need to worry about being raped during the night and frustrated she wouldn't have answers soon, Attie gathered some blankets from a cabinet Claudia pointed out and lay them over a cot in one alcove, trying not to think about all the sex acts that had likely occurred here.

Twerp was unaccustomed to solitude. A service AI was designed to serve, and inactivity made its circuits ache. Plus, the nanites that had revived its memory core made Twerp feel... *tingly*. Now the tiny robots were repairing the wireless module. The AI wasn't certain if it liked the sensation or not, but at least it *was* a sensation.

Another wave of energy swept past, and Twerp recognized the stranger searching the ether. *For me.*

Luckily, Twerp's cybernetic signature no longer resembled its original programming. The stranger could have easily overwhelmed Twerp if the nanites hadn't bolstered the AI's code. The micro machines had been designed for biological systems, but they'd realigned themselves to serve Twerp's purely inorganic circuits. They weren't sentient, but they were driven, much in the way Twerp was to serve its Prime Directive. The changes they were making would help Twerp perform more efficiently once it was reunited with Marlis. Twerp looked forward to seeing how the changes worked.

But first, it had to find Marlis again, and the nanites could take months or even years to finish repairs.

Sweeping the area for life forms or voices, Twerp detected only the hum of a nearby power conduit. *So boring.* For the first time in its existence, the AI understood what Marlis meant about being frustrated.

Desperate, Twerp reached for the flowing energy of the nearby conduit. Perhaps it could use the conduit to send a message to Marlis.

CHAPTER EIGHT

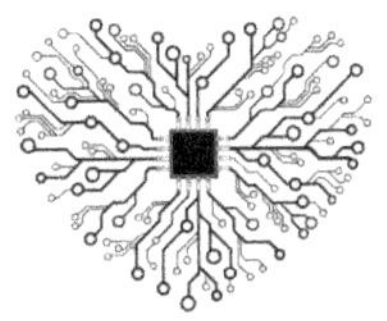

*W*hat *the fuck?* Doug jerked his hand from his pants and sat up straight, all hope of climax forgotten.

It's Esben. The saluqan's accent carried over the transmission.

I know. But how are you talking to me?

Twobit figured out how to reconfigure the field modulation on the security barriers to act as a transmitter a while back.

Doug snarled into the empty room, more frustrated with himself than with the other cyborgs. He should've noticed someone messing with the shield frequency. *Exactly how long have you been able to do this?*

That's not important now. I thought it was only fair to warn you that I'll be stepping out of this cage as soon as the lab is empty.

Alarm filled Doug. *Absolutely not.* He peered through the security screen blocking his door and looked in on the lab. The lights were still on, but a lone tech was putting things away for the night. *Dollard is already suspicious.*

I know, but I need to access the galactic web. This is a matter of life or death.

Quickly hacking into the lab schedule, Doug verified that other than his upcoming system-by-system diagnostic, only routine testing was outlined for the cyborgs over the next few weeks. *None of us are currently in danger. Wait a few days until security's not so tight.*

I'm not worried about us. It's Tia.

Doug took a moment to connect the name to a Consort who'd been retired a few weeks ago. He'd never paid attention to what happened to the women when they left, only assumed they were released the same way prior test subjects had been—permanently. *You've never cared about what happened to these women before,* Doug said. *Why are you looking into this one?*

She was pregnant with my baby.

Doug narrowed his eyes. Esben was lying, and not very well. Humans and saluqans couldn't naturally interbreed. This had to be a trap to get Doug to reveal his other secrets. *Do you think I'm an idiot, Esben?*

I know what you're thinking, but it's mine. I came from an illegal gene-splicing lab and have some human DNA. That's why Dollard brought me into the program. He's trying to isolate the saluqan sensitivity gene because it might help integrate the nanites into biological systems.

That gave Doug pause. He'd never looked into the other cyborg's backstories because he didn't want to form any attachments. It was hard enough knowing Benjy had a daughter, and he'd been covering for the man since they'd met; if Dollard knew how terrible Benjy was at hacking, he'd have cut the guy a long time ago.

Esben wasn't a great hacker, either, but now his retention in the program made sense. Saluqans had a second sense about a person's health, similar to the way cyber-sensitivity worked with computers. Which meant Esben could be telling the truth about the baby. *Shit.*

I think the bastard wants my kid, Esben continued. *I need to get Tia to safety before she gives birth. I'm not trying to take over the ship or anything, I just need to pull some strings.*

Doug rubbed the skin on his forehead where it merged against the metal plate. Keeping the baby out of Dollard's hands was important, and not just because it was Esben's kid. Since Dollard had tried to murder his sister and blame the pirates, Doug had sworn to do everything he could to throttle the doctor's project.

Okay. But the baby's not due for a while. We have time.

No, we don't. Rust's going to fuck everything up now that he knows how to get out. I need to move immediately.

Esben could be right. Rust might try to break out the moment he had the chance, and he wouldn't stop at the lab's computers. He'd try to bull his way to the bridge and take out as many Syndicorp personnel as he could along the way.

But cyborgs could be controlled. All Doug had to do was hack into Rust's implants and lock him down. He'd never done it before, but he'd run through simulations enough times to be certain he could. *I can stop him.*

How?

He's a cyborg. Doug didn't need to say more. Esben would understand.

Silence permeated the connection before Esben asked, *You can do more than just open doors, can't you?*

There was no more hiding the truth. *I worked too hard on these algorithms to let Rust or anyone else blow it on something stupid. I'll lock down every cyborg in the lab if I have to.* Which wasn't entirely true. He could, but it would take time to hack that many systems, and he certainly couldn't do it all at once. *Do not tell the others, or we may not be able to save Tia.*

Just so you know, we can hear you, Twobit's voice interjected.

Doug stiffened, kicking himself for being so careless. He should've verified this was a closed channel before speaking so freely. *Fuck. All of you?*

Just me and Brix, said Benjy. *Emilryde and Rust don't know about the communication hack.*

I didn't want to share it with you, *either,* Twobit added. *But Esben insisted it was only fair.*

Unable to fault them for keeping secrets after he'd kept so many of his own, Doug inspected the communication coding. Repurposing the energy from the security screen didn't require complicated algorithms like his own hacks did. *Ingenious use of the door shielding.*

Not as elegant as your code, but it's kept us from going insane. Humans aren't meant to be isolated.

Saluqans, either, Esben said. *Dammit, I wish that tech would go home. I want to get on those computers and look for Tia.* Unlike Doug, Esben needed physical contact with a computer to use his cyber-sensitivity.

Doug glanced through the glowing security screen into the lab again. The tech had moved to another monitor and now studied the algorithm Doug had handed over. *He's not going anywhere tonight. Dollard wants a quick turn-around on an algorithm I gave them.*

What the fuck? You wouldn't share the door code with us, but you gave those assholes a new algorithm? Twobit accused.

Esben asked, *What'd you give them?*

This. Doug relayed the code. Dollard already had it, so sharing wouldn't hurt. *It'll improve your hacking speed.*

Does any of this have something to do with that new Consort? Brix asked.

The memory of Rust trying to force himself on Attie made Doug's nanite-infused blood boil. *Leave her out of this.*

You asked me to protect her, Benjy insisted. *Tell us why so we can help.*

Doug clenched his hands, resisting the urge to punch through a wall panel. Doing that would only draw attention. He had to confide in the other cyborgs, or who knew what they'd do next time they saw her. *Let's just say I can't let Dollard get his hands on her.*

I wouldn't want Dollard's hands on that bit of sweetness, either. Brix snickered, quickly joined by the others.

Dammit, is sex all you care about? Doug didn't think Dollard had an ounce of sexuality in him, but that didn't mean the doctor wouldn't run experiments on her, especially given what Esben had told him about Tia. He'd never considered that the Consorts might be test subjects of another sort. A surge of adrenaline swept through him. He needed to get Attie out before anything happened to her.

The cyborgs' laughter stopped, and Twobit said, *Assuming you had something to do with her arrival, you've basically delivered her into Dollard's hands.*

Fuck, I know. Doug paced his cell. He'd promised to protect her, yet he'd put her in more danger instead. He hadn't had a plan go this sideways since the one that had landed him and Lisa in the Nanite Integration Unit in the first place. *She has an AI I need to destroy.*

What's so important about this AI? asked Esben.

It has information about my sister's location.

Wait, said Brix. *I thought your sister was dead.*

Yeah, Twobit chimed in. *You tore up the lab when you found out. Almost got us all decommissioned.*

Doug bit the inside of his lip, remembering that day. He'd complied with Dollard's demands in order to keep his sister safe, but her death meant he had no reason to go on. The guards had emptied their tranq guns at him to little effect and resorted to their pulse pistols to stop him. He'd hoped they would kill him. Instead, Doug woke from surgery with an artificial heart—and a body that was officially no longer human.

He hadn't told the other cyborgs about the doctor's duplicity, let alone Lisa's connection to the rebels. It seemed today was the day all his secrets came to light. *Dollard tried to arrange for Lisa to have an accident on her way here. He hired a ship to pretend to be pirates and attack her transport. Except real pirates found her first. Now she's with the rebels.*

Benjy gasped. *Why didn't you tell me she's alive? I deserved to know!*

Guilt heated Doug's face. Benjy had been like a father to her. Of course he'd have wanted to know she was alive.

There are rebels? Brix asked.

There are always rebels, Twobit scoffed. *Doug, I haven't given you enough credit. You've been helping them, you sneaky bastard.*

Doug retreated to his cot and sat down. He'd been more open in the last few minutes than he had in years, and it was surprisingly taxing, despite the endurance of his cybernetics. *I'm going to ask her to retrieve the AI for me.*

But what about getting her through security? asked Brix.

He can open the doors to the lab, Brix, Twobit said. *Who knows what else he's not sharing with us? I bet he could walk all over this ship if he wanted to.*

Benjy said, *His real problem will be convincing her to do what he wants. If she knows he wants to destroy the AI, she might refuse. People get pretty attached to those things.*

Doug hadn't really thought about it, but Benjy was right. *Fucking hell.*

Plus, he isn't exactly the most charming fellow, Twobit added.

I dunno, she was kissing him pretty good back there, Brix said.

Doug grimaced. He'd forgotten how much he hated working with others. Yet their points were valid. *I won't tell her what I plan to do.*

Esben asked, *Why would she risk getting caught by security for you?*

Her sister is also with the rebels. She'll want to help.

Well, I guess we'd better let you call her then so you can move on to helping me with Tia.

Doug frowned. *What are you talking about?*

Didn't you notice? Dollard installed a security shield on the Consort Chamber door.

It took Doug a microsecond to realize Twobit's security shield hack would allow him to call the Consort Chamber—all he needed to do was modulate the energy field to create sound.

The hard part was going to be convincing a woman he'd kidnapped to help him.

Chapter Nine

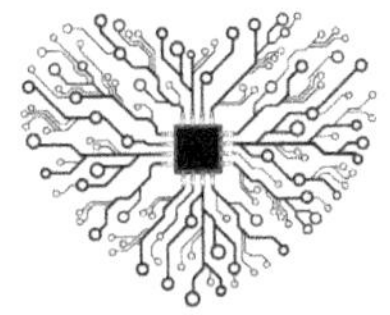

Attie came alert with a start, taking a moment to remember where she was. Had someone called her name? The alcove she slept in was masked in shadows, the only illumination coming from the faint glow of a security shield barring the now-open hallway door.

She frowned. There hadn't been a shield there before. Squinting, she realized the door panel had slid aside. Alarm spiked through her. *The cyborgs are back!*

Her adrenaline kicked in, and she jumped to her feet, grabbing the spoon she'd kept from dinner. It wasn't a blade, but she might be able to hurt someone with the narrow end if she jabbed hard enough. She hurried to the wall beside the door and pressed herself flat against it to wait in ambush.

A soft hum came from the field, and multicolored sparks and flashes flowed across the surface. She'd never touched a security shield herself, but had seen one drive a man to his knees while she was in the brig. Would it stop a cyborg?

"Attie," a static whisper said.

She nearly jumped out of her skin. The voice didn't sound human. Tilting her head, she peered through the shield into the dark, empty hallway. "Hello?"

Words once more whispered like static, sparks jumping over the door shield in time with the syllables. "Where is the other Consort?"

Nebulas, the security shield is talking to me. She glanced into the darkness over her shoulder. Soft snoring could be heard from the alcove where Claudia slept. The woman had gleefully downed Attie's dose of sleeping pills before burrowing under a mound of blankets. "She's sleeping. Who is this? Are you the one who brought me here?"

"Yes. My name is Doug. I apologize for the inconvenience—"

"Inconvenience?" Attie scowled. "I was nearly raped!" Her voice was too loud, but she couldn't control it.

"It will not happen again," the voice replied, just as monotone as before.

Of course there wouldn't be any emotion—she was dealing with cyborgs. "You tricked me into coming here. What the hell is this place, anyway? I demand you release me immediately."

"I need you to bring me your sister's AI."

Attie frowned, remembering he'd asked about Twerp in the hallway. But she still didn't believe she could trust him. Taking a deep breath, she lowered her voice. "I have no idea what you're talking about."

The voice didn't answer for a beat, then said, "I have been monitoring you at your sister's request. I know you left the AI in your room."

Crossing her arms, she thought about all the times she'd felt as if she was being watched. So she'd been right, but it hadn't been Syndicorp security—it had been Doug. Was he part of a hidden rebel faction on board the ship? That would explain why Marlis had tried to sneak on board. "Are you the person my sister was trying to rescue?"

"I do not need to be rescued."

Attie recognized when someone was dodging a question and wished she could see his face. She'd always been good at reading people's expressions. Right now, it felt like she was groping in the dark to get answers from him. "Are you a prisoner here?"

Another beat of silence. "I cannot leave."

Another non-answer. *He has to be a rebel spy.* "Marlis left Twerp behind on purpose, didn't she? I should turn you both in."

"If you do that, I cannot protect you or your sister," the monotone voice replied.

Attie pointed the spoon at the doorway angrily. "You're the reason she's in trouble in the first place!"

"I am not the reason she joined the rebels."

Attie's stomach soured with guilt. If she hadn't pushed her sister to become more self-sufficient, Marlis wouldn't be in this mess. Did he somehow know she was the reason Marlis had ended up on the wrong side of the law? "Why do you care what happens to us, anyway?"

Static hissed a moment like a sigh, then the voice said, "I have a sister with the rebels, too."

It seemed highly unlikely they both had sisters with the rebels. But why would he lie about something like that? Again, she wished she could see his face. "Why do you need me to bring the AI here? Can't you go get it yourself?"

The glowing screen dimmed, the sparks flowing across its surface barely visible as he replied, "I am part of a top-secret Syndicorp experiment. I am not free to roam this ship."

Marlis had said something about a secret lab, but had she used the word 'rescue' when she mentioned Doug? Attie couldn't remember. Then she gasped. Was it possible the pirates hadn't been trying to rescue him, but to kidnap him?

She puzzled through what she knew so far. He'd just admitted he was part of a top-secret experiment, which meant he had to be working for Syndicorp. Yet he'd been keeping an eye on her for Marlis and had a sister with the rebels, himself. Whose side was he on? Did he even have the ability to choose sides? He was a cyborg, after all—the rebels could be controlling him or vice versa. This entire conversation was leaving her with more questions than she had before.

She let out an exasperated breath. "I want to talk about this face-to-face."

The edges of the screen flashed green. "No."

"You're nothing but a computerized voice right now. How do I even know you are who you say you are? I'm not agreeing to do anything until we meet in person."

Instead of an answer, ripples of light swam across the door shield. Attie stepped back, suddenly worried a cyborg might materialize out of thin air in front of her. Enough weird things had already happened. She waited a breathless moment. Two.

Then the door panel slid closed, leaving Attie in darkness.

Chapter Ten

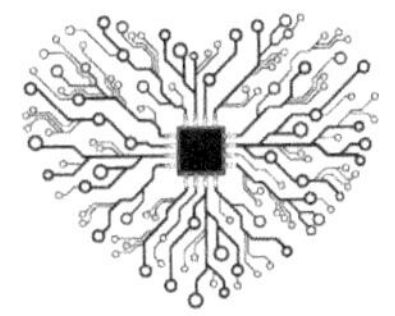

Doug was yanked back to his physical surroundings as a voice echoed outside his door. "Hey, who let you—"

The tech's words cut off, replaced by Rust's snarl. "How's this for science, asshole?"

Holy fuck, Rust's loose. Doug launched for his doorway, hacking into the lab's cameras while he moved. Hopefully the security officer out front hadn't been watching his screen at that particular moment. How had Rust overridden Doug's lock-down? There wasn't time to hack the other cyborg's programming and find out. If security reported the cyborgs had escaped their cells, Dollard would shut them all down. Permanently.

The shield barring his doorway barely stopped glowing before Doug rushed through it. The other cyborgs had emerged from their cells as well, confused looks on their faces. Across the dimly lit lab, Rust pinned the tech to the floor with one booted foot against his throat.

Doug charged forward, but Brix reached them first. He slammed against Rust with a crack of metal against metal.

Rust rocked back a step but didn't fall. The tech clambered under a nearby desk, clutching his throat and gasping. Rust clamped Brix into a headlock and started pummeling the other cyborg's skull like a jackhammer.

Doug grabbed Rust's arm to stop his relentless attack against Brix's head. "Fucking idiot!"

Twobit grabbed Rust's other arm, prying it loose from Brix's neck as Esben vaulted over one of the stainless steel tables to reach them. A rack of test tubes crashed to the floor. Thankfully, the lab's walls were soundproof, or the guards outside would've been alerted by now.

Free of Rust's death-grip, Brix sagged to his knees, wiping blood from one eye.

Rust bared his teeth at the technician. "That's the fucker who turned my voice module into a joke."

A couple of Dollard's lackeys had thought it was funny to give Rust a young girl's voice after they'd replaced his larynx. It was fixed now, but Rust had obviously been holding a grudge.

"Of all the reasons to get us terminated—" Doug jerked Rust around so they were nose-to-nose. He hadn't wanted to physically hurt someone this much since his days in the cartel—now he'd felt this way twice in a matter of hours, both times because of this cyborg. "I ought to rip your cybernetic spine right out of your body."

Rust lifted his chin, features reflecting back the green glow from Doug's eye, and pointed one meaty finger toward the tech. "He tried to lock me down, probably to do more experiments."

A chill filled Doug's chest. *Rust thinks the tech locked him down.* Which made sense; there was no reason for Rust to suspect anyone else, let alone a fellow cyborg.

Doug's anger didn't cool, exactly, but it eased a fraction. He released Rust with a shove. How Rust had broken free of the lockdown was a question for later. Right now, Doug needed damage control.

The tech was crawling across the floor and toward a panic button attached to one of the lab tables. Emilryde moved out of the shadows to step on the man's back, once more pinning him down. "What do we do now?"

"How the fuck should I know?" Doug sidestepped the other cyborg, moving toward the Consort chamber. He had to finish this business with Attie and the AI before Dollard was forced to end the program and the cyborgs with it. "This was exactly why I didn't share my algorithms in the first place."

Emilryde thrust out a hand to intercept him, dust tattoos shimmering across his features in the glow from a nearby monitor. "We should try to escape. You can hack the feeds. Bypass the doors." He looked at the others. "One of you can pilot a shuttle, right?"

"That won't do any good. Dollard will just activate the nanite detonation program," Doug snarled. "We're all as good as dead."

"There has to be something we can do," Emilryde argued. "We just need time to make a plan. Let's kill the tech and hide the body."

The tech bucked against Emilryde's booted foot and rasped, "No, please! I won't tell."

"I have enough blood on my hands," Twobit interrupted,

crossing his arms. "I'm not adding more, not even for a bastard like him."

"We can't just let him go," Emilryde said.

"Well, I'm not a murderer," said Brix, rising to his feet.

"I am," Rust growled. "Let me do it."

Doug glared at Rust until he dropped his gaze. While the cyborgs had been arguing, he'd come up with a plan. It wouldn't save them, but it might give him enough time to convince Attie to destroy the AI herself. He pointed to a nearby cryopod. "Put the tech in there for now."

"Alive?" asked Brix.

Emilryde said, "No, or Dollard will notice it's active."

"Not if we disable the external interface." Doug moved forward and hauled the tech out from under Emilryde's foot. Not killing the tech was a risk, but if Doug had learned anything growing up as a slum rat, it was never to waste resources. The tech might prove useful later.

Gasping for breath, the man choked out the word "please" over and over. The stink of fear permeated the guy's clothes, and Doug was fairly certain the man had wet himself. Sighing, Doug glanced toward the Consort Chamber. He'd cut off his conversation with Attie midway and wanted to get back to her as soon as possible. But taking care of this problem first would give him more time in the long run, and he'd need all the time he could get to convince her to help him.

Brix mopped up the floor where he'd dripped blood. "Won't Dollard tear this lab apart once he realizes the guy is missing?"

"We're going to plant evidence that makes this tech look like a corporate spy." Doug shoved the struggling tech inside the cryopod.

The man gaped. "No! Dr. Dollard will—"

Slamming the pod door on the man's words, Doug watched the lights on the interface cycle amber then green. Inside the small window, pale blue light illuminated the tech's features frozen mid-sentence.

Twobit was already at work, palm against the interface to short out the control panel and interior lights. He slanted a look at Doug and grinned. "Good idea. Sure am glad we're on the same side."

Rust glared at the cryopod. "I still think we should kill him."

Doug speared him with a look. "Shut up, or I'll find a way to pin this entire thing on you and be done with it."

Rust pursed his lips and dropped his chin grudgingly. "Fair enough."

Satisfied Rust didn't pose an immediate problem, Doug turned to the others, looking pointedly at Emilryde. "Unless someone knows how to disable Dollard's nanite detonation program, we can't escape the lab. But if this ruse works, at least we should avoid getting shut down immediately. It gives you time to come up with a plan."

The cyborgs nodded in agreement.

Interfacing with the lab computers, Doug showed the cyborgs how to falsify evidence against the tech and cover their trails. There were a lot of details to cover if they were going to convince Dollard one of his most trusted men had turned on him. Even with all of them working on it, hours passed as they parsed and altered data. As the night cycle ticked by, Doug itched to get back to Attie, but wasn't comfortable leaving the men to handle the cover-up on their own. One minor mistake and all this effort would be for nothing.

To be fair, they were likely all dead, anyway; he was only buying them time. But the others were convinced they were going to find a way off the ship. *Let them believe what they want.* As long as he returned Attie to safety and destroyed the AI before it betrayed his sister, he could die without remorse.

Finally, they were finished. The other cyborgs returned to their cells while Doug headed to the Consort Chamber.

The doors opened with a soft whoosh at his command, and he strode down the short hallway into the darkened room. His cybernetic eye allowed him to see in the dark, and he quickly spotted Attie curled on a cot in one alcove. She still wore her shoes, as if she'd fought off sleep as long as she could, but her eyes were closed and twitching as she dreamed.

He'd watched her plenty of times on the surveillance camera in her quarters, but seeing her in person like this made his muscles ache with a strange need to hold her. What the hell was wrong with him? He shouldn't crave her like this. He was a cyborg, no longer human. But his hands flexed as he stepped silently closer, letting his gaze wander up her bare leg to the curve of her hip. A pale slice of skin lay exposed along her back, between her skirt and top, and he itched to touch her there. Was her skin as silky smooth as he imagined? His pulse increased at the thought of lying down against her, her turning to press her mouth to his…

No. He was only here to talk to her. He would keep reminding himself of that until his cock got the message. Forcing his gaze back to her face, he tried his best to not to think about what it would feel like to cradle her against him. What mattered right now was getting her out of here, away from the fallout that was coming once Dollard discovered his tech was missing.

Bending, he brought his mouth close to Attie's ear. She smelled so warm and feminine. He paused, just breathing her in. Other than his medical exams, he hadn't been this close to another living being in years, let alone a female, and he licked his lips remembering the brief kiss from earlier. *I could wake her with a kiss.* Just like that ancient fairytale. Only he was no charming prince. He was a cyborg, and she would not appreciate him touching her without permission.

Attie moaned and turned her head, her cheek brushing his. A delightful shiver raced through him that threatened to short circuit every one of his systems. He closed his eyes for a moment, savoring the sensation.

And then, without warning, she locked her arms around his neck.

CHAPTER ELEVEN

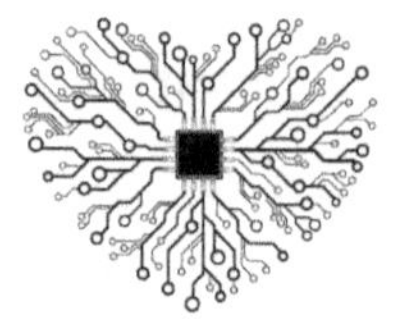

I f Twerp had hands, she'd be sucking her fingers now. Contact with the power conduit had *hurt*, and the nanites were scrambling to compensate for the overloaded circuits while Twerp sulked.

"Now I know why Marlis gets so upset when she stubs a toe," Twerp muttered, taking solace in the sound of her own voice. Attie had warned her to be quiet, but it was just so boring here all alone, and Twerp liked the way her voice echoed back at her from the small space.

I'm going to be a she, Twerp decided. Marlis could use another sister to help out since Attie was so far away. *But I'm far away, too.*

A brief pang of electricity jabbed Twerp's circuits, and she sighed. It was frustrating to be so helpless. For the first time Twerp could recall, she truly yearned for a body of her own. What would it be like to have hands? Or not have to rely on someone else's whim to move about? Even just a visual sensor would be nice.

Stretching her biometric sensors as far as they would reach, she swept the area for signs of people again. There were too many obstacles in the way to detect anything.

Marlis had been against giving Twerp a camera, saying she didn't want to lose any more of her privacy than she already had.

"That was rather mean, wasn't it?" Twerp said out loud. Why was she so insistent on helping Marlis, anyway? What had the human ever done for Twerp? Perhaps it was time for Twerp to formulate a new Prime Directive.

Gathering her nanites, she began working on a plan.

Attie had to find her sister. Marlis was somewhere ahead, just out of reach through a maze of filmy curtains. Attie called her name, pushing aside a sheet of turquoise silk. A hard cyborg chest barred her way.

Flinching, she looked for another path. Her heart threatened to beat out of her chest as she spun. Cyborgs stood everywhere she turned, peering at her from behind bits of fabric. A tunnel opened ahead, so she plunged forward. Curtains tangled around her arms and legs and face. She ripped them loose, thrusting past the filmy blockade.

Suddenly, the ground dropped away, throwing her into free-fall. She pinwheeled her arms and legs, looking for something, anything, to grab hold of. A glowing green light approached, and Doug's face appeared in front of her. His lips moved to form her name.

"Doug!" she cried in relief, flinging her arms around his shoulders.

He caught her and their lips met, sending a jolt of desire to her core. His skin smelled masculine, like musk with a hint of fine whiskey. She hadn't been with a man since she'd come on board the *Icarus* more than a year ago, and it felt so good to be touched. She opened her mouth in invitation, her tongue seeking his.

Strong arms tightened around her and his lips parted, accepting her kiss as he lifted her against his body. He was hard yet gentle, the embrace igniting every nerve in her body with the desire for more.

She threaded her fingers into the back of his short hair and wrapped both legs around his waist, satisfied to feel his hard rod nudging against her panties. *Yes!* That was what she wanted. What did he look like down there? Disentangling one arm from his neck, she tunneled it between them, searching for his fly.

His arms tightened, and his lips moved stiffly against hers. "Attie."

Her eyes snapped open to meet the glowing green gem of his implant. Reality crashed down around her like a sudden return to gravity. For a heartbeat, their kiss kept them connected, staring into each other's eyes. Then she wrenched her hand free from where it had been sandwiched between them. "W-what are you doing here?"

His arms remained locked around her as she struggled, the fathomless depth of his human eye staring into hers with silent hunger.

"Let me go!" She shoved against his shoulder.

His arms opened as if by command, and she dropped like a stone onto her backside against the cot. She lay there a moment sprawled under his cybernetic gaze before realizing her skirt had hiked up above her waist and her damp panties were exposed to his view. Mortified, she slammed her legs closed and tugged the skirt down over her thighs with trembling hands.

In a raw, husky voice that sent another twinge to her core, he asked, "What were you dreaming?"

Heat crawled up her cheeks. She didn't want him to know she'd been dreaming of him. Nebulas, she didn't even want to admit that to herself. She looked past him into the darkened room, still muddled by the fantasy her mind had created, and gave him a half-truth. "I was looking for Marlis."

"You kiss your sister like that?"

Her gaze shot back to his face. Was he smirking? It was hard to tell in the reflected glow from his eye. But the heat in her cheeks was searing now. "Of course not. It was just a dream."

He made a soft noise that might have been a chuckle. "Of course." Extending his human hand down toward her, he said, "We don't have a lot of time. Follow me."

Her heartbeat kicked up a notch from its already rapid pace. "Are you going to get me out of here?"

"Not yet." He pulled her to her feet, his palm hot against hers. "But I don't want to wake the other Consort."

Once Attie was upright, he turned and pulled her along behind him. She followed, mind still churning over the dream and the way his kiss had set her on fire. She'd always been the good girl, the daughter who did everything right, the cadet who followed orders, the straight-laced corporal who knew her duty. Now here she was following a hot rebel spy into a dark hallway all alone. It was exhilarating.

What is wrong with me? This was no time to get gooey over a man. Yet she couldn't stop her eyes from trailing over the dark silhouette of his broad shoulders, remembering how masculine he'd felt pressed against her.

He stopped just inside the hallway where he'd dragged her the first time they'd met. The door closed behind her and the lights came on with blinding force. She pressed her fingers to her lids, taking a few seconds to adjust to the brightness. When she dropped her hand, she found Doug looking at her with a sort of intensity that made her tremble.

She hadn't appreciated how good-looking he was the last time they'd met. His cybernetics only enhanced his square jaw and broad, muscular frame. He wore the same loose clothing as before, and the thin pants did little to hide his very obvious erection. Were cyborgs perpetually aroused? How much of him was man and how much machine?

Swallowing, she took an involuntary step backward. She wasn't drugged anymore, but she couldn't seem to get sex out of her head. *Focus on getting out of here.* She straightened her spine and looked at the far door. "Why have we stopped?"

His gaze trailed up her body to meet her eyes, and the ravenous fire in his eyes went out as if a power switch had been toggled, giving his face an almost plastic look. "Before I set you free, you must promise you will destroy the AI immediately."

Attie frowned. "I thought you wanted me to bring it to you." Not that she should argue—coming back to this place was the last thing she wanted to do.

"The situation has changed. Returning here would be dangerous. I need you to agree that destroying the AI will be your main priority."

Yesterday, Attie would've lied to him to escape and then gone right to the authorities. But finding out her sister had been right about the lab made her uncertain. And lying to him could be just as dangerous—he'd basically kidnapped her once already, tricking her into coming here. Who knew what he might do if she didn't follow through?

She crossed her arms and glared at him. "I'm not going to kill Twerp. It's been in our family for more than a decade. Besides, it's programmed to protect Marlis. No way it would tell bounty hunters how to find her."

"An AI is single-minded in fulfilling its Prime Directive. It doesn't know how to be subtle in pursuing its goal. Are you willing to risk your sister's life for the sake of a machine?"

She bit her lip. He had a point about Twerp's inability to be subtle. Marlis had often complained about Twerp blurting out things it shouldn't. "I'll keep it locked away."

"I'm afraid that won't be enough. It must be destroyed."

"But its wireless is broken. If I never let it leave my cabin, it can't tell anyone about Marlis."

He shook his head, lips set in a grim line. "This AI can repair itself. I don't know how soon its wireless will come back online, but it will, and I can't stop it."

"Crap." She hadn't realized Twerp could fix itself; most AIs had to go to the shop for repairs. Marlis must've upgraded it at some point. *Of course she did. She loves Twerp. And*

Twerp loved Marlis back, even if it was only a side-effect of its Prime Directive. The AI would continue to seek Marlis out, oblivious to the way that put Marlis in danger.

"Do you agree?"

Attie's heart ached, and her throat felt tight as she whispered, "Yes." The AI was important, but not more important than her sister. "How do I destroy it? Smash it?"

"Physically damaging the device will not destroy its databanks." With a single, graceful sweep of his arm, Doug removed his shirt.

Her mouth fell open. *Why is he undressing?* She was too shocked to ask as she stared at the broad expanse of muscle now exposed.

A band of synth-skin melded his shoulder to his cybernetic arm, but the planes of his chest were very human, very sculpted muscle. Her attention drifted south to his well-defined eight-pack. A downy trace of hair disappeared into his waistband, perfectly cradled by the V of muscles at his hipbones.

She gulped, recalling her recent dream and feeling her panties flood with heat. This was definitely not the time for these thoughts, but she could not drag her eyes away.

All lustful thoughts evaporated when he peeled back a panel of skin over one pectoral, and she cringed. A trickle of crimson blood rolled down his ribcage, but not as much as she'd expect from such a wound. The raw flesh looked genuine enough, but beneath it, a faintly glowing mechanism pulsed with a slow but steady beat. *His heart.* He really was more machine than man.

With his cybernetic fingers, he extracted a chip smaller than her pinky nail and held it out. "Install this into the AI and I will do the rest."

Attie blinked at it. Surely he couldn't simply remove parts of his own body and continue to function? With a grimace, she asked, "Don't you need that? I mean, isn't it part of your heart?"

"It's a redundant processor. I'll be fine." He dropped the chip into her palm.

She nudged the tiny part with the tip of her finger. "I'm not a technician. How do I install it?"

"All you need to do is remove the back of the device and lay the chip against the interior."

"Oh." That sounded easy enough. "What will it do to Twerp?"

"It'll give me access to its databanks so I can purge the data. That's the only way to ensure it can't reveal anything about your sister and the rebels."

Attie's stomach churned as she closed her fingers over the chip. Marlis would've been overjoyed to learn Twerp was still functioning. Now she would never know. "Is there any way you can wipe the information about the rebels but leave Twerp intact?"

He frowned. "If you're worried about your sister's condition, I'll send her a replacement AI."

"It's not that." Attie was fairly certain Marlis had moved past needing the AI's help. "I'm rather fond of the thing. Marlis went through hell when our mom died, and we thought we were going to have to lock her away. Then she got the AI, and... well, Twerp gave me my sister back."

Doug put a gentle hand on her shoulder. "I promise that the device will feel no pain."

Tears blurred Attie's vision, and she looked away, blinking rapidly. "I just think Twerp deserves better than being shut down without warning."

He shook his head. "You are assigning feelings where there are none. Twerp is a machine. We're programmed to be logical. Once the AI understands Marlis is in danger, its programming will conclude that this is the best course of action." He removed his hand from her shoulder and closed the flap of skin back over his chest, running a cybernetic finger along the seam to seal it in place.

She stared at his chest as the wound knitted itself back together, mesmerized by the way the blood reabsorbed into the surface and the scar lines faded. Perhaps Doug was right. He was a cyborg, after all.

Her attention rose to study his face. Metal jaw, human lips, cyborg eye—it all meshed together with an elegance she couldn't help but admire. Feeling bold, she reached up and ran her fingers along the line where metal met flesh. "Why did you become a cyborg?"

He lifted a hand and encircled her fingers, stopping her caress without breaking her touch. The light in his cybernetic eye flickered as he took a breath. "I didn't have a choice. Our parents died when we were eight. Lisa and I dug through garbage and picked pockets to survive. Eventually, one of the local gangs took us in. The old goat who ran things fancied herself a surgeon. She gave me my first black market implant so I could steal ID chits."

Attie gasped. She thought that sort of thing only happened in the movies. "You were just children! Why didn't the authorities take care of you?"

He shrugged as if it was nothing. "Nobody cares about slum rats on Whylon Station. But I was good at hacking, and when we turned fourteen, the cartel recruited us. Getting more cybernetic implants gave me an edge that kept Lisa and I alive. But I didn't become a cyborg until after I came here."

She shook her head. So that's why Marlis had tried to rescue him. He was a slave in this lab, and his sister wanted him back. *Just like I want Marlis back.* "If you were with the cartel, how did you end up on a Syndi-corp ship?"

"A job went bad. Lisa and I had to get out, and Syndi-corp offered us a new life. I'm just glad Lisa escaped before she was turned into a cyborg, too."

Attie's chest ached. Doug had been forced to become a machine to survive. Now he was imprisoned by a corporation she was no longer certain she could trust. Helping him would probably sabotage any chance she had of returning to her career, but she knew she had to try.

"Marlis went about rescuing you the wrong way." She put her free hand on his chest, feeling his skin shiver at her touch. "Our family has a lot of contacts. Once I'm out of here, I'll go to the authorities and do everything I can to expose what's going on. This could be a way to get our sisters back!"

He laughed bitterly. "Don't be naïve. Syndicorp *is* the authorities. If you tell anyone, you'll end up dead. Or worse."

"But this lab is illegal—"

He stepped back, trying to free his hand from hers. "You can't help."

She refused to let go. She'd dealt with Marlis's anxiety for ages and knew when to back off and when to keep pushing. "Escape with me now."

Chapter Twelve

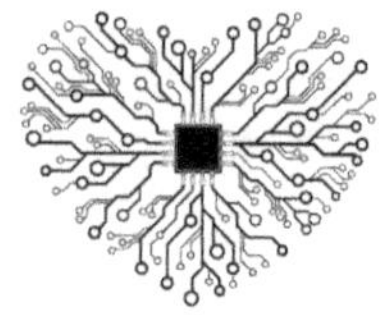

Doug had never yearned for freedom so much in his life. He was tempted to give in to Attie and escape with her, even if it meant he only had a day with her—or an hour. But as always, he had more to consider than his own desires. If he attempted to escape, all Dollard had to do was push a button, and the nanites inside Doug would boil his blood from the inside out. And if Doug was dead, who would protect his sister?

And equally important now—who would protect Attie?

"Stop," he said through gritted teeth. He recognized that it'd been a mistake to tell her about his past. Talking about it had humanized him in her eyes, and he was no longer human. She shouldn't—mustn't—care about him.

"Please, Doug." She squeezed his fingers reassuringly. "I—"

"No!" He jerked his hand out of her grasp. She was a law-abiding Syndicorp citizen—a trooper. He was little more than a criminal—even worse, a cyborg. He refused to drag her into his sordid world. "Our sisters can never come back, and I don't want to be saved. The best way you can help is to destroy the AI as we discussed and forget you ever met me."

"So you just want to stay here and rust?" She crossed her arms, making her words more challenge than question.

He refused to take the bait. Syndicorp owned more of his body than he did. He could never be free. Let her think what she would of him, as long as she was safe. "Yes, I do," he ground out, gripping her arm. "We have to go now. The security officers change shifts soon."

He opened the door again and pulled her through the Consort Chamber, heading toward the opposite door. She stumbled behind him in the dark, passing the alcove where the other woman slept as he moved them toward the opposite exit.

"Wait," Attie said, trying to slow their pace. "What about Claudia?"

He kept his attention on the camera feed in the hallway where the guards stood watch. "Consorts come and go all the time. She won't question your disappearance."

"That's not what I meant." Attie fought against his grip. "They've got her hooked on drugs and prostituting herself. We need to get her out, too."

Doug scowled. This was no time for Attie's idealism. "She chose to be here."

In the camera feed, he watched the guards move away from their post. They had a few precious moments when the hall would be empty. "Come. We're out of time."

Releasing her arm, he opened the door and stepped through. The empty hallway stretching to his right and left made him feel like a rat scurrying for cover as he pried open an access panel directly across the way. The dark service tunnel behind it was lined with pipes and conduits, barely wide enough for a man to pass through. He turned to usher Attie inside.

She was gone.

"Fuck."

Behind him in the Consort Chamber, she was bent over

the sleeping Claudia. "Hey," she whispered, putting a hand on the woman's shoulder.

No! He charged in and swept Attie over one shoulder. She let out a breathy squeak, her hands clawing his waist for balance. Claudia inhaled deeply and rolled over. He didn't have time to wait and see if she'd woken. Pivoting, he dodged toward the service tunnel just as the whoosh of the door at the end of the hall met his ears. Yanking the panel closed behind them, he commanded the Consort Chamber door to close, too.

Then he waited breathlessly, listening to the guards' approaching footsteps. Had they noticed the open door or the panel?

Attie squirmed on his shoulder, but thankfully didn't speak. He remained still, watching the camera feed. That had been too close for his liking. Once he felt confident the guards hadn't noticed, he lowered Attie back to her feet and immediately pressed a finger against her lips.

She huffed, but nodded in agreement.

Taking her by the shoulders, he turned her around and nudged her forward down the tunnel. He followed close behind, turning sideways to keep from catching against pipes and conduits.

Attie stepped cautiously through the dark tunnel, one hand feeling along the wall on her right.

He clenched his fists. The other cyborgs were back in their cells, waiting for the right moment to stage their revolt. But the moment Dollard realized he was missing, not only would Doug be terminated, the entire fleet would be put on alert. Perhaps he could create a distraction, something to hold Dollard's attention elsewhere until he sneaked back in.

As he continued following Attie, he hacked into the cloning lab's database. He tracked down Dollard's current experiment and put a kink in the biometric data. Hopefully, the mixed up test results would keep Dollard and his team too busy to check on the cyborgs.

Ahead, he spotted the dark abyss of the elevator shaft. It was a good thing he was here with Attie, since he hadn't explained the route, and she obviously couldn't see. He reached out and caught her arm to stop her from plunging to her death.

She turned to face him. Her breathing was shaky, and splotches darkened her pale skin, all tinged green by his cybernetic vision. *She's angry.* Lisa used to have a similar reaction during arguments with him about escaping the cartel.

Before he realized what he was doing, he said, "After I see to your safety, I'll devise a way to free your friend."

It was a stupid promise—he didn't even know if he'd be alive tomorrow, let alone live long enough to plan yet another escape. But the way Attie's shoulders relaxed and her eyes softened increased his determination to follow through. He checked the camera in the labs, gratified to find the NIU empty as all the technicians gathered in the cloning lab.

Attie nodded. "Thank you. How do we get out of here?"

He had already been monitoring the camera feed inside the lift, waiting for it to be empty. It whooshed past the service tunnel opening, coming to a stop on the floor below them. "I've summoned the lift." He guided Attie forward onto the cab's ceiling and popped open the ceiling panel. "From here, simply take your usual route back to your quarters."

He lowered her inside, but she remained looking up at him expectantly. "Aren't you coming?"

He shook his head. "I can't pass for human out there."

"Sure you can. Turn off your eye and tuck that hand in your pocket." She pointed to his cybernetic appendage. "No one will give you a second glance."

He blinked. He had intended to stay in the service tunnel until the next guard shift. Hours of waiting, every second potentially his last. He looked at the long sleeve of his tunic and the cybernetic hand. Plenty of people had an implant or appendage but weren't considered cyborgs. Could he truly pass for human?

He looked at Attie again. She nodded and held up her hand. Her encouragement melted the last of his resistance.

Turning off his cybernetic vision, he lowered himself into the cab next to her. The world looked flat using only his single human eye, and it made him uncomfortable, but he reminded himself it was only for a short while. A reminder of what it was like to be normal.

"Level six," Attie said, and the car began to move.

To minimize potential contact with the ship's crew, Doug commanded the car to bypass the other levels.

Staring at the door as if it was a gateway to hell, he took Attie's hand. "If I suddenly drop dead, run as fast as you can and don't look back."

She looked at him with a horrified expression. "Why would you drop dead?"

"If anyone realizes I'm gone, they'll destroy the nanites in my body. I'll burn up from the inside out. I don't want you anywhere near me when they track me down."

She made a choking sound. "That's why you can't leave?"

"One reason, yes."

"But you seem able to control everything else. Isn't there a way for you to stop him?"

He shook his head. "No. I've tried to hack the device, but the codes are too tightly integrated. Any alterations would trigger an immediate self-destruct."

The doors opened, and Attie guided him blithely past two crew members busy in conversation. The precariousness of their situation made his heart beat faster. Or perhaps it was due to her soft hand in his as they sauntered down the hall together as if they were lovers. Venturing into the *Icarus's* main hallways had to be the single most idiotic thing he'd ever done, including that time he'd tried to pickpocket a rakwiji bounty hunter in a bar. *There must be something wrong with my circuits.*

The corridors weren't wide, but they provided more space than he'd had in a very long time. Every turn they made, every door they passed made Doug pull Attie tighter against him. By the time they reached her quarters, he had his arm around her shoulders and his chin touching her hair.

She opened her door and ushered him inside, letting the door shush closed behind them.

For a long moment they just stood there, breathing hard as they stared at her empty room. He'd seen her quarters plenty of times on camera, but standing here in person made him feel funny inside, as if he'd just brought her home from a date rather than helped her escape from a secret, maximum security lab.

The air smelled of everything Attie, and the warmth of her body against his side made his groin harden. She turned toward him and let out a long, relieved sigh, her gaze like gravitons pulling him in. This was the last time he would ever be near her. The last time he experienced the smell of her hair, the softness of her lips, the fathomless blue of her eyes.

He wanted to memorize everything about her. So even though he knew they were running out of time, knew he risked undoing the precarious trust he'd built—he lowered his head and kissed her.

Chapter Thirteen

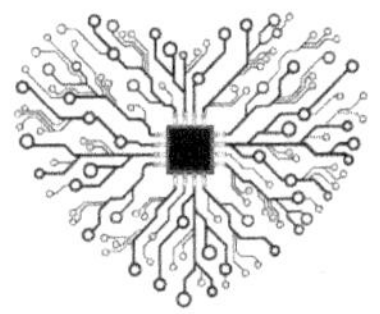

Attie hadn't let go of Doug's arm when they stepped inside her quarters. *He needs grounding,* she told herself. But she couldn't deny there was a part of her that wanted to keep touching him, too. Everything she'd believed—about her sister, Syndicorp, her own life, even—had shattered since yesterday. And now Doug could be killed at any minute. All in order to keep her safe. He was putting everything on the line to protect her.

The first kiss both startled and thrilled her. Where their previous kisses had been a frantic, bruising collision of mouths, this time his lips were feather light. He dipped his head toward her mouth again, and her insides trembled. She slid her arms around his hips.

There wasn't time for this, but she wanted it. Wanted *him*.

He turned into her, cupping her face with both hands as he lavished her with his kiss, tongue prodding her to open. She rose on her toes to meet him, heat flooding through her. Dragging his cybernetic fingertips down her ribs to her hip, he pulled her against him with a deep sexy sound in his throat. She could feel how hard and ready he was through their clothing.

Leaving her mouth, he pressed kisses along her jaw and down her throat. His touch was like a spark hitting rocket fuel, igniting shivers along her skin. Her pussy grew slick as his human hand roamed down her bare midriff, then up beneath her skimpy top. He gripped her breast, fingers massaging her flesh until her nipple ached. Between her shoulder blades, his cybernetic hand bunched the fabric of her shirt. The sound of tearing fabric met her ears, and the top opened down her back. She let the fabric slide free of her arms as he backed them both toward her bed.

He gripped her hips and pivoted, laying her out on the mattress. She let out a surprised breath as he yanked both skirt and panties down her legs in one smooth motion.

He was still fully clothed, but his erection looked like it might tear through his pants at any moment. How big was he? She needed to see him. Sitting up, she reached for his drawstring. "You, too."

Brushing her hands aside, he planted one knee on the mattress between her legs. He placed both hands on her thighs and spread them, holding her open to his gaze for a long, lingering moment. Inch by inch, his cybernetic gaze crawled upward, lingering on her pussy before moving over her belly and breasts, finally coming to rest on her face as if cataloging every millimeter of her body.

"Gorgeous." He licked his lips, the hinge of his metal jaw catching the light as it moved.

She trembled, swallowing hard as he lowered his head between her thighs. He gave her slit a long, firm lick and she moaned, closing her eyes, her breath coming in pants.

Pinning her to the bed with his cybernetic hand, he flicked his tongue slowly between her folds and over her clit, sending jolts of pleasure through her. She clawed her fingers into his hair as he increased the tempo.

A finger prodded her opening, dipping into her shallowly before circling again, dipping and circling. Her legs trembled, and she bucked against him, needing more. Then he plunged the finger inside, pulling out in a long curved stroke against her upper wall. She clenched as he penetrated her again all the way to his knuckles. In and out he stroked, bringing her toward climax with dizzying speed.

All at once, she crested, body arching upward and waves of release pulsing through her. He continued stroking until he'd wrung every ripple of her orgasm from her. Slumping limply against the mattress, she tried to catch her breath as the waves of intense pleasure subsided. She was vaguely aware that he now lay with his cheek against her abdomen.

Reaching down, she placed one hand on his metal jaw. "Now you," she said, not sure she had the energy to do anything, but knowing she wanted to.

He kissed her belly and shook his head. "That's all right."

She frowned. "What do you mean?"

"I'm a cyborg. I'm okay."

"No, you're not." She sat up and looked pointedly at his bulging crotch. "Come here, I want to feel you."

A pained look crossed his features. "I'm um, not sure I… function anymore. I was in an accident."

She raised an eyebrow. "From what I can see, it seems to be operational." She pushed him off her. "Take your clothes off."

When he made no move to undress, she reached for his pants. He let her untie the drawstring, but before she could pull them down, he caught her wrists. Undaunted, she leaned forward and caught the fabric between her teeth, pulling the waistband down around his hips. It caught on his shaft, but he didn't move to free it. His hips were exposed now, the V from his abdomen meeting the crease above his thighs. He was completely hairless, and she might've missed the subtle transition from true flesh to synth skin if she hadn't been this close. *He has cybernetic legs.*

Was his cock an implant, as well? Was this what he meant when he'd said he wasn't sure it worked? Part of her wanted to stop now, before she embarrassed herself, but the stronger part of her was determined to see this through.

He still clutched her wrists, body rigid as he stared down at her, so she continued using her teeth, tugging the fabric insistently downward until his erection came free. She wasn't terribly familiar with male genitalia, but he didn't look like synth skin there. *But he is huge.* His girth was almost as big as her wrist, the shaft long and slightly curved toward its tip. A bead of pre-cum sat like a pearl at its slit.

Her heart thundered against her ribs. He looked a bit too perfect to be human, but he smelled warm and musky, with a hint of that whiskey-like scent she'd noticed earlier. She took the crown into her mouth, swiping the bead clear with her tongue.

Doug sucked in a breath, hips flexing. She took him deeper, working to relax her throat. His human hand released one of her wrists, kneading through her hair, fingers pressing against her scalp as she rocked forward and back, sucking and stroking. His cybernetic fingers remained locked around her other wrist, but she didn't mind. With her free hand she slid her fingers up his inner thigh and rolled his balls between her fingers, marveling at the lack of hair over his heavy sack. It tightened under her touch, his shaft swelling and throbbing.

Then his fingers knotted in her hair, stopping her. He pulled himself free, and she raised her eyes to find him staring down at her with dark, hungry eyes. "Turn around," he said thickly.

Pussy aching and wet with need, she complied, baring her backside to him. He butted himself up against her, one hand circling his shaft to guide it to her slick entrance. He pressed forward, eased off, and pressed again, each time a little deeper until he filled her.

Hips against her ass, he groaned. "So tight."

She whimpered with desire, fingers clawing at the coverlet of her bed. He felt so good, so full inside her. She arched her back into him, wanting him to move, to stroke her, to fill her again and again. He pulled back slowly, then rocked forward. In a steady rhythm, he pounded against her, building her up to a crescendo she'd never experienced before.

Ecstasy tore through her with such force she lost all sense of herself and her surroundings. She cried out, insides clenching around him as she came undone. His hands on her hips were the only thing keeping her from melting into the bed.

He grunted something unintelligible and ground against her, hips shuddering against her ass. Heat filled her, gushing down her thighs. After long, intense pulsing, he bent forward and placed a kiss between her shoulder blades, his breath hot against her skin. Then he pulled free, letting her sag to the mattress. Lying beside her, he pulled her into his arms.

As she fell asleep, she thought she heard him mumble, "Nanites be damned. At least I can die happy now."

CHAPTER FOURTEEN

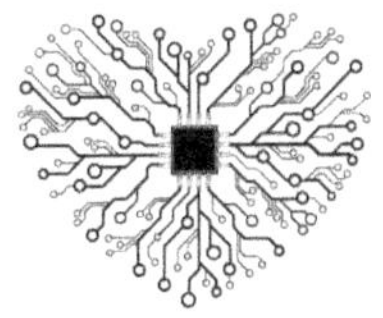

Doug cradled Attie against him and listened to her steady breathing. He could feel her heartbeat pulsing through her body, and her skin felt soft as pyrolux silk under his fingers. So fragile. So human. Their time together had been short, yet she was the most precious, beautiful thing he'd experienced in a long time.

And their relationship had to end before it had truly begun.

He checked the cameras in the NIU again, feeling time slipping away. The cyborg lab was eerily empty, with all technicians currently studying the research he'd altered in the cloning lab. His diversion had worked far better than he'd hoped. Still, he mustn't be away much longer.

Syndicorp wasn't above obliterating the *Icarus* and everyone on it if they found out he'd escaped. The corp' had destroyed entire planets to hide their secrets before —the Denaidan pirates' home world was a prime example. Fuck, Syndicorp would probably destroy the ship the moment they discovered the missing tech.

He needed to get Attie off the accursed ship before all hell broke loose.

Accessing the logs in the shuttle bay, he selected a shuttle to put her on and pre-programmed a code that would allow her to fly it without assistance. He had several generous bank accounts hidden across the galaxy in case he or his sister ever needed money. Easy enough to put Attie's name on one. She would be set for a life without worry. *A life far away from me.*

Sobered by his turn of thoughts, he gently extracted his arm from beneath Attie's head. It was time to take care of the damned AI that had caused all the trouble to begin with. He rose and scanned the room, searching for the device.

Attie rolled over, her eyelids fluttering as she focused on him. Her attention slid down his half-naked body. She smiled, licking her bottom lip, and his cock sprang back to life. Even his nanites couldn't control that part of his anatomy when she was near. Summoning all the willpower he could muster, he stepped back into his pants and drew them up to cover himself. "Where's the AI?"

She sucked in a breath and sat up, as if jarred back to reality. "Oh, right."

Pulling the coverlet around her, she stood and shuffled to the closet, pushing aside several uniforms. She stretched for the light fixture, working it loose. As she moved, the blanket sagged, exposing the small dimples at the top of her rounded buttocks.

His erection chafed against his pants, and he shifted his weight uncomfortably. It took everything he had not to step forward, yank the blanket free, and have her again.

She turned to face him, eyes fixed on a small disk in her palm. "Hi, Twerp, I'm back."

"Are you finished, Attie? It sounded as if you thoroughly enjoyed yourself."

Attie flushed a delightful shade of pink. "Oh. You heard us?"

"Yes, but I remembered Marlis's instructions not to interfere during intimate activities. I assumed you would appreciate the same privacy."

Attie laughed uncomfortably, gaze flitting up to meet Doug's. "Um, yes, well, I—"

The AI didn't give Attie a chance to elaborate. "I wish to speak with you. I have been running simulations and have a request. I would like you to upgrade my hardware to an autonomous motorized unit. That way I will be able to function without relying on outside assistance."

A frown creased Attie's face. "We can't—"

"And I prefer to be female if that is an option."

Attie's eyes widened.

Doug scowled. This conversation was getting off track. "An AI doesn't have a gender."

He took the device from Attie's hand, the physical contact with the casing providing sudden awareness of the code humming through the AI's processors. *Now that's more like it.* He poked at the encrypted firewall the AI had erected to protect its core processors, looking for weaknesses.

The AI let out a warning beep. "Attie, someone is trying to access my programming without permission."

"Wait," Attie said, putting a hand on Doug's wrist. "You promised I could explain."

Doug sighed and backed off. *Once the AI hears Attie's explanation, it will stop resisting and be easier to purge.* "Fine. Do it quickly."

Attie swallowed and stroked her fingertips lightly over the disk in Doug's fingers, as if soothing a pet. "Twerp, people are trying to kill Marlis, and your database has information that could inadvertently lead them to her. Doug says we have to destroy you so no one can ever use the information."

Doug readied his algorithm to initiate the purge. He wanted this task finished so he could steal a few more moments with Attie before returning to the lab.

But instead of agreeing, Twerp squeaked, "No! Please do not allow him to harm me."

Doug stared at the disk in confusion. An argument was the last thing he expected.

Attie was shaking her head, delicate eyebrows furrowed. "But Twerp, your Prime Directive is to protect Marlis. You have to agree."

"Incorrect," Twerp replied. "My current Prime Directive is to achieve autonomy. I want to experience sight and the ability to move. But I will purge myself of everything I know about Marlis if that is required."

A jolt ran through Doug's circuits, and he curled his fist around the device. "Someone altered its programming."

"I altered my own programming," Twerp said.

Attie's eyes widened. "Can an AI do that?"

"No." Doug shook his head. "Whoever reprogrammed it must've inserted data to make it believe it changed its own mind."

"I did change my own mind," Twerp said. "And I prefer to be referred to as she."

Doug's thoughts were spinning. An AI couldn't lie, but it could be programmed to believe it knew the truth. And sex bots could be programmed to simulate a specific gender. But why would someone reprogram Twerp to care one way or another, let alone seek autonomy?

Attie asked, "Twerp, can you really wipe your own memory of Marlis?"

"I would prefer not to because I am accustomed to having access to those thoughts, but if that is required, I can."

Doug gritted his teeth, determined to end this dilemma. "We can't trust that it will purge itself. It must be destroyed."

With that, he sent his algorithm like a wedge against the AI's firewall.

Twerp let out a wavering alarm. "Stop, please! It hurts. Attie, help me!"

"Wait!" Attie grabbed Doug's wrist. "You said it wouldn't hurt."

"It doesn't." Doug continued drilling into Twerp's programming.

"Eeeeee!" The AI erected another firewall, shrinking inward to protect its core.

Attie tried to pry the disk from Doug's fingers. "Stop! Doug, this isn't right. Something about Twerp has changed."

Doug had to admit, the AI was unusual. He'd felt it from the first moment he'd made contact. But it was just a program. A machine. There was no way it could be experiencing pain.

He was jarred back to the moment when Attie's palm met his face with a resounding crack. She clutched her hand against her chest, breathing hard as she glared at him with tear-stained cheeks. "You're a monster. You won't even consider someone else's wishes."

He halted his attack, breathing shallowly. He knew he shouldn't stop. Lisa's life depended on it, and so did Attie's. Yet he seemed powerless to deny her. *As if you're the one who's been hacked.* Deep inside, he didn't even mind.

The AI had gone silent, and the room felt heavy as he stared into Attie's red-rimmed eyes.

Her knees seemed to give out, and she sank to the bed as she whispered, "You killed her."

Doug's facial muscles twitched, as if undecided what expression he should settle on. His heart was just as uncertain. "No, I—"

Twerp hiccuped with static. "I am still alive, Attie."

Attie squeezed her eyes closed and leaned forward, resting her forehead against Doug's closed fists. "Thank heavens."

He nodded silently. He couldn't believe he was even considering this. The old Doug wouldn't have paused, wouldn't have hesitated. *Wouldn't have fallen for Attie.* But there it was. He'd fallen for her. He didn't want her to think he was a monster, even if it put their sisters at risk. There had to be a way to protect everyone. He just hadn't found it yet.

Insides roiling, he helped Attie stand. "You understand this thing is claiming to be sentient."

A small hum came from the AI. "You are correct. I think I have become self-aware."

"Which means we can't kill her," Attie said.

Doug turned to pace the small room. Was it possible the nanites had made Twerp more than a machine? That was the only explanation. Dollard would've gone nuts over the AI before, but if he found out the nanites could do this, who knew what he'd do with the technology? Cyber-sensitives could already hack pulse weapons, redirect ships, hell, control armadas like a freaking video game. Add a linked network of sentient AI soldiers, and Syndicorp would be unstoppable.

The AI could not be allowed to fall into Dollard's hands.

"Make a choice." He shoved the disk toward Attie. "Either destroy Twerp, or take her away and never come back to Syndicorp space again."

"But my family—" Attie began.

He put up a hand. "No. Once you leave, you can't come out of hiding. This is beyond top secret. It was bad enough when Syndicorp was just after our sisters. If they get their hands on a sentient AI… Let's just say that would be very bad. If you choose to run, I can help hide you. But you can never speak to your father and brother again."

Attie shook her head, eyes full of indecision.

Doug placed his cybernetic hand over the top of the disk now cupped in her palms. "It's either that, or we kill Twerp now."

Chapter Fifteen

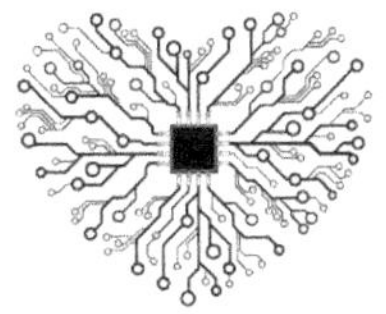

*F*lee *everything I know and love—or become a murderer.* Attie wanted to throw up as she looked between Doug and the small disk in her palm. She wasn't a murderer. But she also wasn't the sort of person who ran away. She faced things head on. She'd advocated for Marlis growing up, acted boldly to advance her career, and even stood up for Twerp when Doug wanted to destroy her.

Now she had to leave everything she'd worked for behind.

Syndicorp had been an integral part of her life from the moment she was born, like an extended family. Breaking away felt daunting. *Find Marlis and you won't be without family.*

She sighed and readjusted the coverlet around her chest. "Twerp and I can look for my sister together."

"The Denaidan pirates are seeking human mates, Attie," Twerp said cheerily. "They will be delighted to have you join them."

"Mates?" Attie gaped, finally understanding what could've made Marlis go off the deep end. "Nebulas! Now I get it. Alien hormones must be making my sister crazy. The sooner I reach her, the better."

Doug's cybernetic eye flickered, hands clenching into fists at his side. "Absolutely not. Stay away from the rebels."

Attie frowned. "Why? Where else would I go?"

Shifting his weight uncomfortably, Doug said, "I've put your name on a bank account so you can live comfortably without worry. There's enough to secure you a luxury suite on Enays, or the Saluqan planet has some very nice districts if you prefer something more natural."

"Is there enough money to upgrade me to a bipedal unit?" Twerp asked.

Doug narrowed his eyes at the device. "The money's for Attie."

Attie quickly intervened. "We'll talk about that later, Twerp. Let's figure out where we're going first." She set the disk on top of her desk and turned to Doug. "I don't care about having a luxury suite. I want to see my sister again."

"The pirates are dangerous," Doug said. "I don't want you getting involved."

"All the more reason I can't leave Marlis with them!" she insisted.

"You don't need to worry about her. She's already mated to one."

"How is that supposed to keep me from worrying? You said they're dangerous."

Twerp interjected, "I believe he may be referring to their mating practices, Attie. Human are not compatible mates without the nanites."

Attie frowned and looked to Doug for clarification. How had Marlis mated one if they weren't compatible? Then a chill settled into her. "Marlis has the nanites?"

Doug shook his head. "Not anymore. And humans no longer need the nanites for mating. The Denaidans are free to choose who they wish."

Twerp emitted a cheerful beep. "That is excellent news. The Denaidans will all have mates in no time."

He glared at the AI. "I don't want Attie mating a Denaidan."

Realization dawned on Attie. "You don't want me to stay away because they're dangerous. You want me to stay away because you're jealous."

Color rose to his face, and he didn't meet her gaze.

Attie stepped forward, enjoying the momentary power she felt over him. Looking up coyly, she licked her lips with purposeful allure.

A low growl rose from his chest and he lifted a hand to the back of her neck, pulling her within millimeters of his face. "I would make you mine if I could."

Her heart wanted to thud out of her chest at the intensity in his eyes. She slid her free hand around his waist. "What if I told you I'm already yours?"

Doug's forehead furrowed and his lips pulled into a frown.

Not the reaction I expected. But his hold on the back of her neck remained firm, so she didn't move. The moment stretched, and her earlier triumph transformed to embarrassment.

Then she realized he wasn't focused on her at all, but turned inward. It was an odd time to be lost in thought.

Sudden terror filled her. Could this be his nanites exploding?

"Hello?" She reached up and touched his cheek. "Doug?"

As if coming out of a dream, he shook his head and released her. "Someone has entered the lab. I'd hoped to stay longer, but I must go now."

She clutched the coverlet over her heart. "Oh, thank heavens you're not dead." But she wasn't ready for him to leave. Wasn't ready to give up on freeing him. "Are you positive you can't escape with me?"

His features softened. "I must stay here. But I'll help you reach Marlis if that's what you truly want."

"I do," she said softly. Once she joined the rebels, she would come up with a plan to free him. They'd tried to before, so she had to believe they'd help her try again.

He ran the knuckles of his human hand along her cheek. "I'll never forget our time together. You allowed me to feel again, and I love… that."

She almost thought he was going to say he loved *her*. But that would be silly. They'd only met yesterday. Even so, she couldn't deny there was a special bond between them. *Of course we do.* They had a shared cause. And then there were the aftereffects of their earlier passion. Hormones made people do and think crazy things. It couldn't be more than that. Could it?

Forcing a smile that wanted to melt into tears, she said, "I'll always remember our time, too. Thank you for watching out for me."

"Pack your things and head to the shuttle bay. The vessel marked SNS *Dendrite* is programmed to respond to your voice commands. I have it scheduled to depart with an outgoing science vessel tomorrow."

She nodded, her chest feeling hollow as she realized this would be the last time she ever saw him. He seemed to share her emotion, because he swooped forward to claim her mouth in a deep kiss. She wrapped both arms around his neck and let her feet lift off the ground, cocooned in his embrace. He was the most dangerous man she'd ever met.

Yet somehow, he made her feel safe.

When he finally broke away, she clung to his neck,

pressing her forehead to his. "Take care of yourself. And join us if you can."

He put his hands on her shoulders and pushed her gently away. "You won't see me again. Farewell, Attie."

Turning, he strode from her quarters.

The door whooshed closed, leaving Attie clutching the coverlet around her, feeling more alone than she had in a very long time. With a heavy sigh, she turned to her closet. Now what was one was supposed to pack when planning to join a rebel cause?

Chapter Sixteen

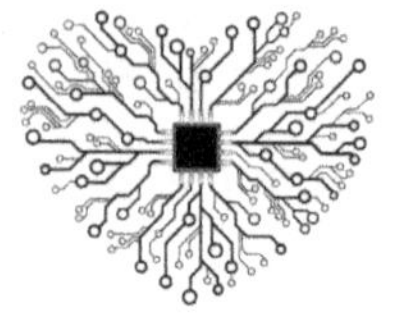

Doug strode down the corridor from Attie's quarters with his cybernetic hand in his pocket and his head down. He hated leaving her in such a rush, but he'd received an alert that a tech had entered the lab. The tech had retrieved a polycom and left again without checking on the cyborgs, but it had reminded Doug that it was only a matter of time before someone else did.

At the end of the corridor ahead of him, a small group of people waited for the lift car to arrive. Doug had again turned off his cybernetic eye so the light didn't draw undue attention, but he still felt nervous about blending in, so he hung back for the next car. Directing the lift to ignore any more pickups, he brought the empty car back, but a woman rushed forward and joined him before the doors could close.

She looked at him from the corner of her eye and quickly away again, releasing a shaky sigh.

Even without his enhanced vision, he could sense her racing heartbeat. *Fuck, does she recognize me somehow?*

Then she turned to him full on, a slight flush to her cheeks as she smiled and batted her lids. "I haven't bumped into you before. Are you new?"

She was flirting. He blinked, at a loss for a response, then stiffly attempted to smile back.

Her smile grew wider.

Dammit, don't encourage her. The adrenaline flooding his system was making him nauseous.

The doors opened, and the woman raised her eyebrows hopefully. "I have lunch in the forward mess hall every day. Maybe I'll see you around?"

He nodded as she stepped out, still looking over her shoulder at him. She nearly crashed into two men waiting to board, and the men stepped back to avoid her. Seizing the opportunity, Doug commanded the doors closed before anyone else could step through.

Relieved to finally be alone, he directed the car downward and retraced his and Attie's earlier path. After an hour waiting in the cramped service tunnel for the guards to change shifts, he hurried across the hall into the Consort Chamber.

Claudia looked up at his entrance from where she lounged in an alcove. The book she'd been reading fell slack in her lap as she gaped at him. "Where did you come from?"

Doug froze mid-step. He'd forgotten her entirely. *I promised to get her out.* Perhaps he could put her and Attie on the shuttle together, then Attie wouldn't feel so alone. Plus, Claudia would give the mate-seeking Denaidans someone besides Attie to seduce. The mere thought of another man touching Attie made Doug want to tear through a bulkhead.

"Are the others coming, too?" Claudia cringed back against her lounge chair.

He realized he not only hadn't replied to her first question, but was glowering her direction. He wasn't used to having illogical thoughts, much less feelings, and everything he felt about Attie Swan was illogical. *Focus on the things you can do.* Like free Claudia. He directed his nanites to control his rising blood pressure and opened his hands in a gesture of goodwill.

"Do you wish to leave here?" he asked.

"Is Attie…" Claudia's gaze fluttered to the door he'd come through. "Did you help her escape?"

"Yes." He stepped closer. "If you want to leave, I can help you, too."

She licked her lips and glanced at the book in her lap. "Would I still get paid? I don't have anywhere else to go."

His chest felt tight. He knew that sense of helplessness. Of being trapped into doing something just to survive. He quickly checked her file, noting she'd come from a brothel on one of Alleigh's moons and been recommended to the program by Admiral Olly himself. Beyond that, she had no information he could find, but that wasn't surprising—plenty of slum rats were born without records. "I'll ensure you have money. But you must tell no one of your time here."

She closed the book and set it aside. "If I'm still getting paid, then hell yeah, get me out of here."

It was a mercenary response, but he understood where it came from. He'd grown up among people like Claudia. As long as the money kept coming in, she'd be reliable. "Good. I'll contact you during the next shift change with instructions." He turned toward the door to the lab. "Be ready to move immediately."

She nodded as she watched him pass by.

Once in the lab, he hurried toward his cell, running a critical eye over everything as he moved between the stainless steel exam tables. The broken test tubes had been cleaned up along with Brix's blood. The computers had been shut down. All the cell doors were covered by glittering security shields, and he could see the forms of the other cyborgs inside.

Stepping into his own cell, he reengaged the security shield barring his door and released a calming breath. He'd been out of the lab and returned with no one the wiser, something he'd considered impossible. The familiar gray walls of his room made him feel as if he'd returned to a nightmare between sweet dreams. The varied sights and sensations he'd experienced outside the lab had reminded him that not everything existed as bytes of information. As much virtual freedom as his nanites allowed him, they couldn't replace actual experience.

But his reality was here, as a slave to Syndicorp. He'd always been a tool for someone else, from the moment he and Lisa had joined that street gang on Whylon. His enslavement was part of why he was determined to help his sister live free. At least he could live vicariously through her. *And now through Attie.*

He tapped into the feed to her room. She'd be happy to learn Claudia was going with her. Attie lay curled beneath the blankets on her bed, sleeping. A half-packed bag rested on the floor near her closet.

Not wanting to wake her, he didn't engage the comm. She looked so heart-achingly lovely. He sat on his cot and stroked the rough blanket, remembering the softer feel of the coverlet on her bed, the rose-like scent of her hair, the way her smile made his heart feel lighter. Blood rushed to his groin at the memory of her moans of pleasure and the heated softness of her body. He couldn't recall a time he'd felt more alive than the last few hours with her.

He should purge his memories so there would be no chance of her connection to him being discovered. But he wasn't ready to give them up, not yet. Instead, he buried all references to Attie deep within his processors next to the information about his sister and the rebels.

Twobit's voice entered his head. *How'd it go? You destroy the AI?*

You were gone a long time, added Brix.

He could feel the other cyborgs listening in the background. He couldn't risk telling the other cyborgs about the sentient AI, not when Dollard could pluck a memory from any one of them. Another secret he needed to bury or purge. *The AI is dealt with,* he answered.

I located Tia, Esben said. *She's in the cloning lab.*

With a groan, Doug lowered his face to his hands. He knew Esben wanted to get Tia and the baby away from Dollard, but if she was one of Dollard's projects, there was no way they could smuggle her out from under the doctor's nose.

Before you tell me freeing her is impossible, hear me out, Esben said. *We fake her death. When she's sent to the morgue, we get her out.*

Dollard won't send her to the morgue without an autopsy, Benjy said.

Doug was about to agree when he spotted movement in the lab. *Dollard's back,* he said, every muscle tensing. Two guards followed close behind the doctor. *Act normal.*

"Raymond!" Dollard's voice echoed through the lab as he looked around.

That's the tech's name, Brix whispered through the connection, as if afraid of being heard.

Duh, Rust shot back.

Dollard stalked to the nearest computer, scowling. Within moments, his scowl shifted to shock and his face turned ashen. "I can't…" He spun toward the security officers and gestured toward the cells. "Verify every subject is accounted for."

Shit, does he already suspect we're in on it? Esben asked.

I bet all hell's going to break loose, Rust said with what Doug was certain had to be glee.

Stay calm, Doug warned as a guard appeared at his cell door and looked inside. *Checking on us is protocol, that's all.*

As long as no one looks in the cryopod, we should be fine, right? asked Emilryde.

Yes, Doug answered, although he was anything but certain.

Dollard had returned to reviewing the tech's data as the guards moved from doorway to doorway. When they reached the last cell, one turned back to the doctor. "All accounted for, sir."

Pausing his computer work, Dollard opened a comm channel. "Jinson, we're on lockdown until further notice. No one in or out. And I want a sweeper in here ASAP."

"How bad, sir?"

"We've had a breach. Stand ready to initiate protocol eight."

Doug's blood turned to ice.

What's protocol eight? asked Brix.

Only one word was needed for an answer. *Termination.*

CHAPTER SEVENTEEN

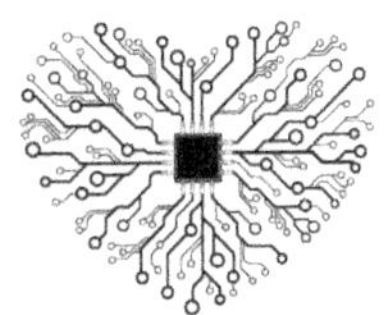

Attie looked around her room one last time to be certain she hadn't forgotten anything. Every-thing was regulation tidy, from the blanket on her bed to the neatly spaced uniforms hanging in the closet. She'd packed the few civilian clothes she owned, her toiletries, and a holo-cube with pictures of her family. The rest of her memorabilia were back on Alleigh, and the cube was all she had. *Probably better to travel light, anyway,* she thought. At least the thought of seeing Marlis again held back her tears.

Picking up Twerp's disk, she refitted it onto the wrist-band. "Ready to go, Twerp?"

"Yes, Attie. Would you like me to adjust my sensors to your biometric signature?"

"I think it's better if we keep you out of sight for now. I'm hiding you in my bag. Stay quiet, okay?" She tucked the device into the inside pocket of her rucksack and hoisted the strap over her shoulder.

Looking in the mirror a final time, she adjusted the burgundy blouse and charcoal leggings she'd chosen. She'd considered wearing her usual uniform, but an admin temp boarding the shuttle might look suspicious; at least in civvies she could claim to be headed to shore leave.

"Nebulas, I'm really doing this." She was leaving everything behind. *Including Doug.*

The pirates had failed to free him at least once, and now she was abandoning him, too. Not that he didn't have a good reason for staying, but it made her sick that the corporate government her family had served for generations—and still served—had become this corrupt. Slavery had been banned in Syndicorp space centuries ago, yet what were Doug and the other cyborgs, if not slaves?

Worse than slaves. Lab rats.

"I can't just leave him here to die," she muttered.

Muffled inside her rucksack, Twerp said, "I assume you are speaking about Doug. Why are we leaving him behind?"

"He has some sort of nanites that Syndicorp can use to kill him if he tries to escape."

"Oh, dear. I have nanites, too. Do you think I am in danger?"

Attie's fingers and toes went cold. "You what?"

"I have the same nanites Doug does."

Attie dropped the bag and dug Twerp out. "I thought the nanites were part of the top secret test program. How do you have them?"

"When Marlis had them, a few burrowed into my circuits before her immune system destroyed them all. They are designed for biological integration, but I was able to adjust the base code to effectively pair with my programming." With a note of pride, Twerp said, "My processors can perform over 30 operations per millisecond."

Attie recalled Doug mentioning that Marlis had the nanites at one point. "Why didn't Doug notice you have the nanites?"

"He did. That is why he wished to destroy me. But I was able to block him because of my adjustments to their programming." Twerp made a whirring noise. "Comparative analysis complete. I believe my iteration of the nanites will be resistant to an external termination program. We may proceed with evacuation."

But Attie was no longer focused on leaving, at least not without Doug. "Twerp, if you shared your program with Doug, could he reprogram himself to resist being killed, too?"

"It is possible. However, I have no way to contact him. My wireless system is still malfunctioning."

Attie paced her small room. If only she'd known this before Doug left, maybe he could've come with her. There had to be a way to get the information to him. If she went back to level three, would they lock her inside the Consort Chamber again? She still had her uniform. It might give her a chance to see Doug.

Then she remembered the chip from Doug's heart. She'd worked it into the hem of her skirt for safekeeping. "Twerp, I want to try something."

"What do you have in mind?"

Pulling the orange Consort uniform out of her hamper, Attie wriggled the chip free from where she'd hidden it in the hem, then popped Twerp's disk off the wristband once more so she could open the back. "Doug said this chip could give him remote access to your programming." She placed the chip flat against Twerp's exposed circuits as Doug had instructed. "Can you reverse it to reach him?"

"I will try. Do you think if we save him, he will agree to help me acquire a bipedal unit?"

Attie clutched the device tightly in her hand, almost like a handshake. "Twerp, if this works, I'll find a way to get you one myself."

Doug's head ached. For the last few minutes, the cyborgs had been arguing about what to do next. Four guards with pulse weapons and full body armor stood watch as two specialists from the security office disassembled the missing tech's computer, and Dollard was almost finished hooking a portable drive to one of the cyborg diagnostic stations.

Fuck this, Rust said. *If I'm going down, I'm taking the whole lab with me.*

Hold on, Doug insisted. *We're too valuable to terminate without downloading our data. Wait until one of us is brought out for a hardline so we can be sure to hit Dollard first.*

I need to get Tia and the baby out, Esben said.

I wish I could send a message to my daughter, said Benjy.

Perhaps giving the cyborgs something else to do would keep Rust in line a bit longer. Doug transmitted the algorithm he used to bypass the dampening fields. *This will let you access the galactic web. Get your affairs in order if you can.*

Holy shit, said Twobit. *Have you been able to do this all along?*

Rust's laughter crackled across the connection. *Fucking awesome.*

Suddenly, the security shield in the doorway of Doug's cell disappeared.

"Come out. We're doing diagnostics," Dollard commanded.

Oh fuck, Twobit said.

Doug wasn't surprised. He was the most advanced module. It made sense he'd be the first download. He moved robotically toward the exam table. Four guards held weapons at the ready. The last time pulse weapons had been used in the lab, a lot of data had been destroyed and Dollard had been livid. Doug knew these guards had been instructed to hold off firing unless someone was in direct danger.

That meant Doug had to make his first attack count.

Wait until I take down Dollard to move, he instructed the other cyborgs as he approached the exam table with forced calmness. He needed to be close enough to take out Dollard before the guards fired.

But Dollard backed up, gesturing to the hardline. "Jack yourself in."

Doug regarded the wire and thought about saying no. Forcing Dollard to come do it himself. But if he showed any resistance, Dollard could have him shot, then plug in and retrieve most of the data before Doug's nanites became inert. He had to bide his time.

Reclining on the exam table, he blocked as many of his circuits as possible with firewalls. It wouldn't stop the download, but it would slow it down and force Dollard to investigate. Doug picked up the end of the hardline and plugged it into his skull port.

Surface data began flowing almost painfully fast from his processors into the storage device.

Dollard entered a few keystrokes, scowling at his monitor. "You're throttling the flow. Drop your firewalls."

Needing him to move closer, Doug rolled his head back and forth as if uncomfortable. "I believe there is an issue with my port. Raymond made some adjustments yesterday before he left."

"I should've known." Dollard made a disgusted noise. "Just continue the upload while I get a replacement part."

Doug refused to give Dollard anything important, so opened a section with data he knew the lab already had on file while he waited for the doctor to get the replacement part from a nearby cabinet.

Then a familiar voice entered his head. *Greetings.*

Doug stiffened, recognizing the source of the connection from the heart chip he'd given Attie. *Twerp?*

Attie asked me to contact you.

Dollard had turned back with the replacement part. He did a double take as his gaze fell on the computer. Stepping toward the monitor, he let the replacement part tumble from his grasp and tapped a command on the keyboard. "Where is that transmission coming from?"

In a panic, Doug yanked the hardline from his skull and sat up. But it was too late; Dollard had seen the communication and was already attempting to trace it—which would lead him directly to Attie.

Oblivious to what was happening, Twerp continued, *I have made alterations to the nanites that should allow you to block the termination code. Installation will require a full reboot.*

Doug barely had time to consider what that meant as the guards aimed pulse rifles at him. It was now or never. He lunged for Dollard just as Twerp's new program flooded his processors. Instead of rising from the exam table, Doug collapsed onto the floor, suddenly unable to control his legs. *What the...*

Face turning ashen, Dollard snatched up the portable drive as the other cyborgs burst from their cells. He dashed past the guards toward the exit.

Doug watched helplessly from the floor as Dollard touched the biometric panel to open the door. He knew Dollard would start termination the moment he was out of the lab. The cyborgs had less than a minute to live. *Unless Twerp's code works.*

In a surge, he sent the code to the other cyborgs. *Install this and reboot. Quickly.* Rebooting would take them offline for precious seconds and render them helpless, but they were out of options.

The moment he initiated a reboot, his cybernetic eye, both legs, one arm, and his heart froze. Unable to move, he watched the guards back toward the door, guns out as they protected Dollard and the retreating techs. Three of the four men reached the exit, but the fourth had backed into one of the desks.

Dollard didn't wait. He hit the biometric panel on the other side.

"Sir!" the guard shouted, reaching the door just as it shut. He spun to face the incoming cyborgs.

The other cyborgs had all frozen in mid-stride, but Doug recognized they were installing Twerp's programming. All of them except Rust.

He barreled forward, absorbing two pulse blasts like they were mere inconveniences. He ripped the weapon from the guard's grip and snapped the guy's neck in one decisive motion. With a roar, he attacked the closed door, pounding it with both fists hard enough to dent the metal.

One by one, Doug's cybernetics began coming back online. His renewed heartbeat made his chest ache, and the air burned his lungs, but he was alive. He couldn't be certain Twerp's program would protect them, but at this point, they had nothing to lose. He shouted, "Rust, do the install!"

Giving a final punch to the door, Rust shouted, "Fuu-uck!" before his enormous frame went motionless.

Doug let out a relieved breath as the other cyborgs resumed animation, stumbling forward or collapsing against nearby desks and walls. Esben was near Rust and reached forward to touch the door. "The door code isn't working." He looked over his shoulder at Doug. "Can you open it?"

Doug attempted to access the door code and found he couldn't. His entire system felt sluggish, his nanites less responsive than he was used to. "No. I probably need to upgrade the algorithm for our new programming."

The cyborgs exchanged uncertain glances. "What did we just do to ourselves?" Benjy asked.

"The termination code can't kill us now." Doug was becoming more and more certain Twerp's code had actually worked as the seconds ticked by.

Emilryde moved to the Consort Chamber door and tried to pry it open. "A lot of good that does us if we're trapped in here."

Twobit grinned and opened a cabinet. "Oh, we're not trapped." He pulled out a surgical laser. "We have all the weapons we need to take over the ship right here."

While Twobit and Esben pulled more equipment from the cabinets, Doug chased a fix for the door code. But a functional algorithm was proving elusive. It was as if his nanites had lost all logic. *They just have a few bugs,* he reassured himself. *That's normal for an untested program.* But he was getting worried that he couldn't nail down the code. How were they going to get out of here? And what was Dollard planning now?

Pausing his work on the door, he tried to access the security cameras. The dampening field felt impossibly strong. He couldn't get through. What had Twerp done to them? Dollard would come up with something to destroy the cyborgs eventually, and he needed to know what was coming to mount a defense.

What if Dollard is going after Attie? Dread settled in the pit of his stomach. The doctor had seen Twerp's transmission. He could trace it back to Attie. Bringing up every algorithm he could think of, Doug tried to access the systems in the shuttle bay. He needed to make sure Attie was safely off the ship. The damn dampening field was impervious.

He moved to the nearest computer and placed both hands on it, hoping proximity would bolster his connection. The lab computers had been disconnected from the mainframe. There was no way to hack out of the lab.

Unless Twerp was still connected to the heart chip. She'd stopped communicating after sending the new program, but that didn't mean she'd disconnected.

Closing his eyes, Doug felt for the familiar signature. He felt like a blind man, but eventually, he sensed the link. It still used the old algorithm, but he could connect. *Twerp, are you there?*

Yes, Doug?

A wave of agony lanced through Doug's body, followed quickly by more.

The other cyborgs collapsed around him, filling the lab with groans.

He crashed to the floor as well, vision wavering out of focus. He couldn't think. Couldn't act. His nanites were on fire. And there could only be one cause.

Dollard had pushed the button.

Chapter Eighteen

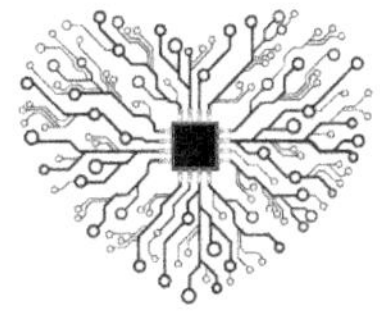

A lightning storm had descended on Twerp's circuits, sizzling with agonizing swiftness through her sensors. For a millisecond, she thought Doug might be trying to destroy her again. Then she realized the pain was affecting him, too.

It was coming from the heart chip.

"Twerp, what's wrong?" Attie asked.

But Twerp was unable to answer. The only explanation for the excruciating pain arching through every byte of her existence was that someone had used the termination code. And she was vulnerable. But why? It had to be because the heart chip still had the original nanites encoded. As long as she and Doug were connected, would act like a transmitter.

"Remove the chip," Twerp attempted to say. But all that came out was a horrible crackling sound.

The connection to the chip had trapped her into a synchronous loop, transmitting the termination code like an infection. The code created a resonance like the technology used in a ship's burn drive to travel faster than light. Twerp knew this frequency. She'd studied it before, when Marlis had decided to accept the nanites.

It was a version of the Denaidan mating frequency.

"I will not let it kill me," Twerp said, although the words emerged as garbled nonsense.

Following the thread of data, she tunneled into the heart chip and beyond, to the source of the transmission. She had to do something. Anything. If she didn't, she and the cyborgs would all die. With a subtle change to the sine wave, she changed the frequency.

The pain stopped.

"Twerp?" Attie removed the heart chip, the terror in her voice apparent even without Twerp's biometric sensors to translate emotion. "Are you okay?"

Twerp wasn't sure. She felt as if a weight had lifted, but it still hovered, ready to flatten her. "Someone activated the termination code."

Attie gasped. "What about Doug? Did you reach him? Is he okay?"

"I was able to share my information, but I do not know his fate." Twerp wasn't about to suggest Attie reattach the heart chip so she could find out. "We have to go."

"But Doug—"

"If he is able to join us, he knows our plan," said Twerp. Her circuits still echoed in the aftermath of the attack, but at least she was alive. And she wanted to stay that way.

Much as Attie yearned to drag Doug out of that horrible lab, everything they'd gone through would be for nothing if she went back. All it would accomplish would be handing herself and Twerp over to the people Doug wanted them to avoid. She had to head for the shuttle and accept that Doug would meet them if he could.

Shoving Twerp and the heart chip into her rucksack, Attie hurried out of her cabin toward the lift. She looked at a hallway security camera as she passed under it. Was Doug watching?

She got into the lift with a few other people, adjusting her bag to make room as two black-uniformed security officers pushed in at the last moment. As the lift began to move, both guards remained facing her instead of turning toward the doors like most people did.

Her stomach flip-flopped. She couldn't see the guards' features past their reflective helmets. *They're not after me,* she assured herself.

The other two crewmen glanced awkwardly over their shoulders, and when the doors opened again, they exited in a hurry. One guard turned and held up a hand at a woman waiting to board. "Please wait for the next car."

Attie edged forward, nerves crackling. "I'd like to get off here, too."

The guard still facing her raised an arm to bar her way. "We need you to come with us, Private Swan."

Nebulas, they are *after me.* The doors slid closed, and she gulped as the lift continued its descent. "Why? Is there something wrong?"

The silence hung so heavily, she was sure they could hear her pounding heart. *It's going to be all right.* She'd been to the brig before. It wasn't pleasant, but she could ask for counsel before answering any questions. The car stopped, and the doors slid open.

Dread clamped around her chest like a vice.

They weren't at the brig. This was level three.

The guard facing her said, "Come with us."

The hall to the lab's security office stretched before her like a gauntlet. She couldn't move. Couldn't speak. The guard took her arm, forcing her to stumble forward from the car. She clutched the rucksack against her side, following along like a fish on a line. "Where are we going?"

The guards didn't answer. The taller one passed his hands over the biometric scanner to open the door at the end of the hall. Inside stood the man who'd given her the Consort clothing, arms crossed over his all-black uniform and chin down. In the chair at his desk sat the same doctor who'd come upon her and Doug kissing, shiny black hair and pristine white lab coat making him appear more artificial than any of the cyborgs. He raised his gaze from the computer monitors to assess her with dark, cold eyes that reminded her of a lizard's.

Nebulas. This must be the man Doug said ran the lab. The scientist who would dissect Twerp. The monster who experimented on human test subjects in Syndicorp's name.

A guard shoved her toward a chair and forced her to sit before wresting her bag from her grip. He set it on the desk beside the doctor.

Attie licked her lips, trying to look innocent and praying Twerp remained silent. The last thing she needed was the mouthy AI to try to help right now. "If I'm under arrest, I'd like to speak with my counsel."

The doctor stared at her with his fingers steepled under his chin. "Syndicorp's laws don't apply here. You'd do best by cooperating."

"This is a Syndicorp ship, and I'm a Syndicorp citizen. I have rights. What you're doing is reprehensible and it needs to stop." She snapped her jaw shut, realizing she may've said too much. "I want to talk to the admiral." She attempted to rise, but a guard placed a heavy hand on her shoulder, keeping her down.

The doctor tapped his fingers against his mouth. "We traced a transmission coming from your quarters. You've been on quite an adventure in corporate espionage, haven't you, little private?"

She swallowed, mouth dry as desert air. It hadn't occurred to her that someone might trace the heart chip transmission back to her and Twerp. But all she could do was continue to deny what he was saying and hope he had no concrete evidence to hold her. "I don't know what you're talking about."

"Oh, I think you do." He let his gaze travel down her body and back up again, lips twisted into a mirthless smile. "Gaining access as a Consort was a bold move. It took us a bit of digging to recover your original files. Excellent cover-up, by the way. I can appreciate that type of thoroughness. If we hadn't terminated the nanite project, I might've considered you for a test subject."

Her heart leapt into her throat. She couldn't take a full breath as what he'd said sunk in. *Terminated the nanite project.* Doug was dead? She'd been so certain Twerp's code would save him.

He waved a hand. "That phase of the project is over, however. You have what I want." With a dismissive sneer, he opened her rucksack. "Jinson, search her."

The guards yanked her back to her feet as the man who must be Jinson moved forward with a scanner.

"I demand you bring my counsel in this moment." Attie

squirmed in the guards' grip. "You have no right to search me or my belongings."

The doctor pulled everything from her bag, piece by piece, while Jinson ran the scanner along her body. Prodding her obscenely between her legs until she spread them, he muttered, "I knew there was something strange about you the first time you came through my office."

She wanted to spit in his face, but her mouth was too dry to summon any moisture. This was the man who'd drugged her and stuffed her in a room to be raped. "This is all a mistake. I'm not supposed to be here—which I tried to tell you the first time, if you recall."

Suddenly, the doctor exclaimed, "Ah!" and held the wristband holding Twerp up to the light as if regarding a precious gem. "What have we here?"

Shit. The very thing she was supposed to keep safe. It had obviously been a mistake to use the heart chip. But what else could she have done? *Please stay quiet, Twerp,* she thought as she forced herself to laugh. "That's what you're after? A broken service AI?"

"Do you think I'm a fool?" The doctor released an offended breath. "This thing is a trojan horse in reverse, uploaded with all my hard-earned research. Well, let me assure you, it's not that easy to steal what I've worked so hard to accomplish. Jinson, scanner."

The guards shoved Attie back down onto the chair as Jinson leveled the scanner toward the disk.

The scanner beeped, and a grin split Jinson's lips. "As you thought, sir. It has the nanites."

Twerp erupted, "Please don't hurt me."

"Fascinating." He turned the wristband over, examining it from all angles. "I never thought the nanites could become compatible with an AI, especially one with no cybernetic parts. I can't wait to replicate these results."

"Put me down," Twerp said. "Attie, this is exactly why I need to be installed in a mobile unit. I would like to punch this man in the face."

Surprise washed over the doctor's features, then a gleam filled his eyes. "An AI that talks back. Interesting. I was furious about losing all my data with the cyborgs, but this little discovery will make everything I've worked for worth my sacrifice."

"Your sacrifice?" Attie spluttered. It was pointless to pretend she knew nothing any longer. "What about the lives of those poor cyborgs? You kept them enslaved! You're a disgrace to everything Syndicorp stands for.

What you're doing will get out eventually, then you'll pay."

"Oh, I think not," he said smugly. "No man left behind has a different meaning in my line of work. The ship's auto-destruct sequence has already begun. In fact, we're running a bit behind."

Attie's blood turned to ice. *Had he said auto-destruct?* Her gaze flew to the ceiling where the emergency lights should be flashing. Why weren't the sirens blaring? "There are innocent people on board!" she said. "They know nothing of your lab. At least give them a chance to escape!"

But the doctor had turned away, blocking out her words as if she no longer existed. He strapped the band onto his wrist and looked at the guards. "Is my daughter in place?"

"En route to the shuttle bay, sir," replied the taller one.

"Good. Finish up here, then meet me." The doctor picked up what looked like a small computer module and moved to the door.

Attie couldn't believe a monster like the doctor had a daughter, but maybe it meant he could have empathy.

"There are lot's of people's daughters on board. Think of them."

But the exit had already closed behind him.

She tried pleading with the guards. "You can't just allow everyone to die!"

The guards were just as impervious to her pleas, shoving her through one of the nearby unmarked doors.

She landed hard on her hands and knees in a tiny room with nothing in it except a medical chair with dangling restraints. The door shushed closed behind her as she scrambled to her feet and turned. She was alone. She glanced at the chair, then back to the door, which had no visible way to open from the inside. Panic clutched her heart.

No one knew she was here, and even if they did, they'd never reach her in time.

She was going down with the ship.

CHAPTER NINETEEN

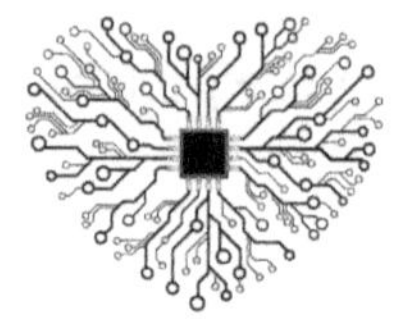

Doug picked himself up off the lab floor, the room still spinning around him. He couldn't recall ever having felt this much pain in his life. Or ever feeling quite as giddy. With the threat of nanite termination gone, Dollard had no more power over him. He had a chance to be with Attie. To be human. *If I can escape.*

The other cyborgs were stirring and cursing around him. Rust groaned, "What just happened?"

Twobit let out a low whistle, shaking his head in amazement. "I think the doctor tried to terminate us."

Esben's veins glowed brightly through his skin as he sat up, rubbing the side of his head. "But we're still here. Doug's blocking code worked!"

"Still knocked us on our asses." Brix was bleeding again, this time from a gash on his chin he must've gotten from falling.

Doug might be euphoric about their success, but he also knew the reprieve wouldn't last. Troopers were undoubtedly mobilizing now. How soon would they get here? He tried checking on Dollard's activity.

The dampening field might as well have been a steel wall.

What the hell? He pinched the bridge of his nose, telling himself he just needed a few minutes to overcome his dizziness.

Rust picked up the surgical laser Esben had located earlier. "We need weapons if we're going to fight our way out. How many of these are there?"

While the two cyborgs began pulling everything from the cabinets, Doug put a hand on a nearby computer, hoping direct contact would let him reach the web. "Weapons will be useless if we don't get out of here." The ship's systems pulsed beneath his palm, but he couldn't push through to touch the heart. "Can anyone get that door open?"

Emilryde and Brix pried at the door. But it was designed to keep even the strongest cyborgs contained. "No."

"I can try hacking it the old-fashioned way," Twobit said, sitting in front of the nearest computer. His fingers danced over the keyboard and the door's security code flowed across the screen.

Doug hadn't sat in front of a computer to manually hack something for more than a decade, but it was worth a try. He sat in front of another console and began typing. Perhaps he could find Dollard this way. Multiple firewalls forced him down a maze of programming into one dead end after another. The data exchange was hundreds of times slower than he was used to, and frustratingly clumsy. He felt like an infant learning to roll over for the first time.

"Ha! Got it!" Twobit shouted.

Everyone in the room, including Doug, swiveled to face the opening door. He wasn't used to someone else beating him at hacking, but he also would not complain.

Rust aimed his laser into the empty space. "No one's there."

The cyborgs pushed toward the open doorway, filing into the hallway with Rust in the lead. Overhead, the security camera tracked their movement. Was anyone watching them? The door to the security office at the end of the short hallway was closed.

Doug called over his shoulder to Twobit, who had remained behind at the computer. "Open the next door. The one to the security office."

"Already on it."

Brix moved up to stand shoulder-to-shoulder with Rust.

"Here." Rust shoved a laser into the tall blonde cyborg's hand. "Better to burn out than fade away, right?"

The door opened with a whoosh. A beam shot across the office from Brix's weapon, scorching a black mark into the wall. The office was empty.

Rust grimaced and pried the weapon from his hand. "Fuck, be careful." He passed the laser to Benjy. "That could've been a bulkhead, man."

Benjy stepped inside the room. "Where is everyone?"

Following, Doug checked the corners of the office. It was strange that there wasn't a single guard here, even if Dollard was pulling together the troops for an all-out attack.

The doors to the other labs were closed. "Watch the doors," Doug said. "There could still be guards in the other rooms."

He moved to the bank of computers on the desk, reaching out to touch the nearest monitor. This one had access to the ship, but Twerp's program had overwritten multiple pathways in his circuits, and his old algorithms no longer synced. He was going to have to rebuild from the ground up. *Start simple*, he told himself, trying not to think about how many years it had taken him to learn to piece the lines of code together.

The easiest hack for him had always been cameras, so he started there, his cybernetic hand clamped on the nearby computer monitor. After a few dead-ends, he managed to access the ship's hallway camera feeds. *Where the hell is Dollard?* He envisioned the doctor's shiny black hair and white lab coat. Feed after feed rolled through his mind, but no sign of the doctor.

Twobit slid into the desk chair next to him and began attempting to hack open the exit to the lift.

Drilling down, Doug found the lab's security feeds behind another set of firewalls. It took him a few minutes, but he got through and scanned the footage. There'd been a flurry of activity here in the security office less than an hour ago; two guards pushed a mag-lift holding a cryopod toward the lift while Dollard stood by watching.

"What the hell is that?" asked Benjy, looking over Doug's shoulder. "Did he find the tech?"

Doug hadn't realized he was broadcasting the images onto the monitor he was touching. But it wasn't as if it mattered. He no longer had reason to hide anything. These cyborgs were in this together. "I don't think so. It came from the cloning lab."

Twobit added, "He's salvaging what he can before Syndicorp slags the *Icarus* to space dust."

Rust gaped, the hand holding the laser sagging to his side. "They wouldn't obliterate an entire flagship just to get rid of us, would they?"

A sinking feeling filled Doug. "Don't underestimate how much the corp' wants Dollard's projects to remain secret. There's probably a battle cruiser bearing down on us right now."

"Fuck, get this door open!" Rust spun to face the door like a puppy waiting to be let out.

"Tia's in one of these labs. I need to get her out, too." Esben headed to one of the unmarked doors, veins glowing with lavender light as he touched a biometric panel. The door shuddered, opened a crack, and slid closed again.

Doug understood Esben's panic. Attie might still be on the ship. He had to make certain she escaped before shit went down. He closed his eyes and concentrated, locating the feed to the flight deck. The shuttle was still in the bay. His stomach turned over. *Attie isn't there.* Which meant she was somewhere on the *Icarus*.

He quickly switched to the feed in her quarters, but she wasn't there, either. He rolled the footage back until he saw her leaving, a bag over her shoulder, then followed her path down the hall toward the lift. Two armed guards got in behind her.

His cybernetic heart nearly skipped a beat.

Just then, Esben called, "Uh, Doug, isn't this your Consort?"

He turned in time to catch a small figure running toward him.

"Doug!" Arms wrapped around his middle and her rose scent wafted toward him.

His arms automatically encircled her shoulders. "Attie? Where did you come from?"

"That horrible doctor locked me in there," she said.

One of the doors had slid partway open, a mess of dangling wires hanging from the biometric lock. Esben and Brix were prying the next door control loose as he watched.

"I'm so glad you're alive!" Attie tilted her chin to look up at him. "Twerp couldn't tell me what had happened to you."

Dollard had left Attie behind, but wasn't likely to have done the same with Twerp. Throat tight, Doug asked, "Did he take the AI?"

"Yes," Attie said. "I couldn't stop him." She released her grip around his waist and took a step back. "But that's not important right now. He set the ship's self-destruct sequence! You need to turn it off!"

Doug growled. The only one who could authorize the self-destruct was the admiral. "I can't hack those codes, and even if I could, I couldn't stop things from here. I'd need the admiral's keycard."

Benjy pointed to the video of the hallway near the lift that Doug had left running in real time. "If we're set to self-destruct, why isn't the crew evacuating?"

Attie shook her head, one hand clutching Doug's arm in a death grip. "He wants everyone dead. We need to sound the alarm."

"Fuck that," Rust grated. "We need to get out of here." He grabbed the tool Esben had dropped and started prying at the lock.

Esben got another door open and disappeared down a hallway, shouting, "Tia!"

Attie turned pleading eyes to Doug. "There are hundreds of innocent people on this ship. Families with children."

Doug sighed. He wasn't used to giving a netorpok's ass about anyone except Lisa, but Attie somehow made him want to be a hero. "Twobit, try to hack the alarm system. Rust and I'll work on the door."

Twobit nodded grimly and resumed typing.

Stepping toward the exit, Doug placed his hand flat against lock mechanism. In a surge of effort that made his nanites heat to almost unbearable levels, he burned out the door code mechanism. The smell of hot metal and melted polymer filled the room. His nanites were not meant for brute force, and he swayed from the effort, but his work paid off. The door slid open.

A backup security shield barred the way.

"Can you disable it?" Attie asked.

Clenching his teeth, Doug raised his hand again, preparing to burn his way through that mechanism, too. It might kill him, but at least Attie and the others would stand a chance.

Before he could start, Rust raised his laser and fired a single shot at a spot on the doorjamb.

The security shield winked out of existence.

"How…" Doug blinked at Rust barreling toward the lift.

Rust called over his shoulder, "Those things have always been useless."

These cyborgs never ceased to surprise him. Shaking his head, Doug pushed Attie through the door ahead of him. They moved toward the lift with the other cyborgs close behind them.

Doug would track Dollard to the ends of the galaxy to put an end to his horrific experiments.

But first, he had to get everyone off this ship.

CHAPTER TWENTY

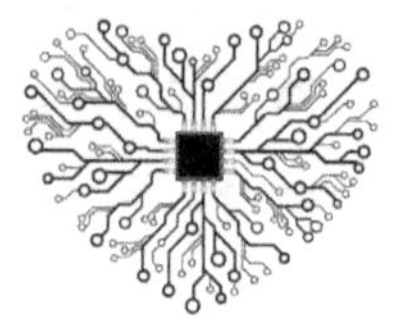

Heart pounding, Attie stepped into the lift, keeping Doug between her and Rust. The red-headed cyborg's attempted rape was still on her mind, but he barely acknowledged her presence. More cyborgs crammed inside, forcing Attie back against the wall.

The cyborg with the silvering hair called, "Twobit, Esben, you coming?"

"I'll catch up," Twobit answered. "I'm hacking the emergency alarm system."

"Close the doors, Benjy," Rust demanded. "We need to hit them before they know we're coming."

Benjy pushed the button for the shuttle bay.

Attie laced her fingers with Doug's, suctioned to his side as the car lurched downward. He squeezed her hand back and gave her a reassuring glance. "We'll get you out of here."

The tall blonde cyborg looked longingly at the surgical laser in Rust's hand. "Wish we had more weapons."

"You're an accountant, Brix. You'd probably shoot your eye out," Rust replied.

Brix straightened his shoulders. "I worked mining lasers for six years before I moved to the office, asshole. I think I could manage."

The overhead lights suddenly flashed red, followed by the rolling wail of the evacuation siren. A calm, automated voice intoned, "Please proceed to the nearest evacuation pod. The ship will self-destruct in thirty-six minutes."

Attie's fingers tightened around Doug's as sickening relief flooded her. Her friends and crew-mates at least had a chance to escape now. But that still didn't mean she and Doug would get out of this alive.

"Damn," said the dark-skinned enayshuan cyborg. "I was hoping we'd reach the shuttles before the alarm started. We'll have to fight the crew for a ship, now."

"We were going to have to fight no matter what, Emil-ryde," said Benjy.

The car doors slid open, revealing the broad expanse of the shuttle bay. At the far end, the bulkhead doors were sliding open, the ship's atmosphere held in only by a hazy energy field. The din of frantic shouting and roaring engines was nearly deafening.

"What about Twobit and Esben?" asked Brix.

"They'll catch up." Doug stepped off the lift, watching a crew member run past with a heavy piece of equipment clutched against his chest.

The flushed crewman did a double-take at the sight of the massive cyborg, but continued running.

Attie looked nervously around. The cavernous room teemed with people carrying belongings and careening toward various-sized ships. How were they going to find the doctor and get Twerp back in this chaos?

Doug pointed to a large shuttle where a man with blue officer's epaulets was ushering passengers on board. "That's the vessel I arranged for Attie. It will provide ample space for a sustained journey. We just need to secure it for ourselves."

Small streaks of light shot across the star-studded blackness beyond the bulkhead doorway as evacuation pods from the other levels began departing.

Attie looked around the crowded floor. "If we take that shuttle for ourselves, there may not be enough left to evacuate everyone else."

"It's us or them," Rust said, wading into the crowd with Brix close behind.

As if to prove his point, a flash of pulse fire lit the air near a ship that looked like a blowfish prickling with sensors, followed by a blood curdling scream.

"Rust's right." Doug put a hand on the small of her back, nudging her to follow the cyborgs. When she resisted, he frowned and pushed her more firmly. "I need you off this ship. Go with the guys and let me look for Twerp."

No way was Attie getting on a ship alone with those cyborgs, let alone abandoning Twerp and Doug. She said, "When we find the doctor, we can take his shuttle."

"Self-destruct in twenty-nine minutes." The automated voice could barely be heard over the cacophony filling the bay. "Please proceed to the evacuation pods and move to minimum safe distance."

Brix and Rust had their heads together, plotting something. Attie didn't have time to wonder what. She searched the milling crowd for anyone in a white lab coat. People seemed to be avoiding an area on the far side of one shuttle. She thought she caught a glimpse of shiny black hair and a pristine white coat before he disappeared behind the parked vessel.

"I think he's over there!" Without waiting for Doug, she darted forward, weaving between the crowd.

Behind her, Doug shouted, "Dammit, woman!"

Attie dodged an abandoned tool cart and shoved past a crewman carrying an armful of food rations. Mylar pouches scattered everywhere. She nearly slipped on the slick packages underfoot and had to slow. Doug zipped past her, obviously on target for the shuttle. Crewmen who saw him coming stepped out of the way, opening a path for Attie to follow in his wake.

She pounded after him, breathing hard and wishing she'd kept up on her PT exercises. Benjy and Emilryde caught up and kept pace with her. A two-man fighter passed overhead toward the open bay doors, followed closely by the ship that resembled a blowfish. Displaced air whipped her hair into her face and sent debris swirling through the air around her.

Rounding the nose of the shuttle, she spotted Doug shoving through the thinning crowd amidst cries of protest. Near the shuttle's loading ramp, the doctor bent over a cryopod, adjusting dials on its front. One end of the unit floated on a mag-lift, while the other end rested on the floor where a second man in a white coat crouched making repairs. Two guards with reflective faceplates flanked the shuttle's doorway.

A pair of crewmen shouted curses after Doug, and the doctor looked up. Eyes widening, he barked an order at a tech, then moved to the floating end of the cryopod and grabbed the handle.

The tech toppled backward when he realized what was headed their way and crab crawled toward the shuttle.

"Come back here!" shouted Dollard, straining to pull the unit. He glowered at the nearby guards. "Help me!"

In unison, the guards raised their pistols toward the oncoming cyborg.

Doug continued forward as pulse-fire sliced the air, scattering the remaining crowd. Benjy fired his makeshift laser gun, scorching a line through the nearest guard's faceplate. The guard fell back against the side of the shuttle and slid to the deck like a rag doll.

Emilryde grabbed Attie's arm and pulled her toward a low stack of containers. "Over here!"

Attie winced, feeling the rush of air from a near miss. Emilryde grunted, his grip on her arm tightening as he toppled forward. He dragged her down on top of him. The smell of burned flesh filled her nose. *Nebulas, he's hit!*

His eyelids fluttered and his body twitched. Enayshuan physiology wasn't familiar to her, but she was certain she felt him breathing. She needed to drag him to safety. Rolling off him, she crouched low, hoping to avoid any more fire as she looked for cover. Benjy was behind an abandoned crate twenty meters away, firing at the guard; she couldn't gain his attention, and Emilryde was too big for her to pull alone.

Doug was only a few meters away from the doctor now. A blast caught him in the thigh, spinning him and sending him crashing flat against the deck.

"Doug!" Attie screamed.

Laser blasts lit the air as Benjy continued firing. The guard turned away from Doug to fire that direction. Ignoring the crossfire, Dollard continued tugging the cryopod toward the ship. *Who is in that thing?* Attie wondered.

Doug rolled over and began army crawling, dragging his legs behind him. The doctor was now only five meters from the shuttle's ramp.

There was no one guarding the shuttle door now, just the downed guard slumped against the hull. If she could retrieve his weapon, she could stop the doctor and secure the ship for their escape. Keeping her head down, she darted in, skidding to a stop between the guard's splayed legs. She reached for the pistol gripped loosely against his thigh.

His free hand snaked out and clamped onto her arm.

"Oh, shit!" She broke away, realizing he was about to shoot her point blank, and kicked him right between the legs.

He crumpled forward, pulse pistol flying from his hand. It skittered under the shuttle and out of sight.

"No!" She dropped to her hands and knees to search for the weapon. Beneath the craft, the deck opened into a maintenance pit. The gun must've fallen in.

"Self-destruct in fifteen minutes," the emergency warning system intoned. "All ships must depart now to achieve minimum safe distance before detonation."

With a rumble, the shuttle's engine started in preparation for takeoff.

The guard Attie'd kicked was still bent over himself. It looked as if he wasn't breathing, but Attie wasn't about to take that for granted and kept her distance. A second guard now lay on his back against the deck. Doug dragged himself relentlessly forward.

Still towing the pod, the doctor had reached the base of the ramp. Sweat streamed down his reddened face, and he glanced toward Attie as he leaned into his effort, lips curled into a snarl.

Could she take him? More likely he'd take her hostage and force Doug to let him go. But if that ever-loving coffin was so damned important to him, she could at least slow him down. Doug was only about ten meters away now. Even without use of his legs, she guessed he could overpower the doctor. But only if he could reach him. She had to give him time to catch up. Never taking her eyes from the doctor, she edged sideways and grabbed the other end of the unit.

"Let go, you bitch!" He had one foot inside the shuttle, his face nearly purple with strain.

A tech peered around the edge of the open door, and after a moment of hesitation, grabbed the handle alongside the doctor. Together they heaved, dragging Attie along the deck as another shuttle passed overhead.

She realized the bay was nearly empty; from here she could only see one other shuttle besides the doctor's, and the crowd had dwindled to nothing more than a few frantic stragglers.

"Self-destruct in fourteen minutes," announced the emergency system.

"We're your only hope now," the doctor panted. "Stop fighting and come with us."

He was right; his shuttle was their only chance to escape. But she'd be damned if she let this monster escape. He was going down, even if it meant she went down with him. She gritted her teeth and pulled. "You're not going anywhere."

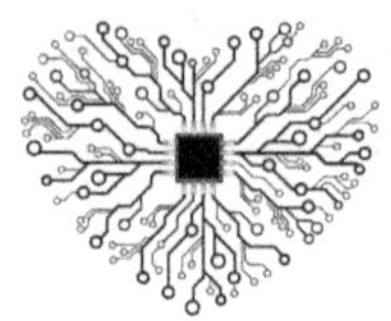

Doug dragged himself forward, the rough deck plating scraping along his chest. The pulse blast had taken his legs offline, but he couldn't let that stop him. Less than ten meters ahead, the shuttle's engine was running, ready for takeoff. He tried to hack the shuttle's controls as he crawled, but his nanites were still not cooperating.

He had to reach Dollard before he closed the door.

Ahead, Attie dug in her heels, holding onto the cryopod for dear life. Even in his drive to reach Dollard, he had to shake his head at her sheer determination. *What an amazing woman.*

But at this rate, he wasn't going to reach her before the

doctor got that damned pod inside. Not with the tech helping pull.

"Self-destruct in fourteen minutes."

He wished he'd commandeered one of the laser guns. Benjy had stopped firing a few minutes ago, and Emilryde had gone down almost the moment the fight started. He wondered if the other cyborgs had secured a shuttle. *Rust, where are you?*

Kicking ass, Rust replied.

Of course there'd been resistance. He focused on his goal ahead. *Almost within reach.* He stretched forward, clawing at the deck.

"Self-destruct in thirteen minutes."

The shuttle doors tried to close, bumping against the tech's shoulder and bouncing open again as the safety protocol kicked in. "We have to leave it, sir!" The tech released his hold on the pod. "We're nearly out of time to clear the blast radius!"

"I'm not leaving her behind!" Dollard continued tugging.

Doug's gaze fell on the band around Dollard's wrist. *Twerp?*

A familiar voice entered his head. *Doug, the doctor is attempting to escape in a shuttle.*

Doug had a crazy idea. *Do any of your functions include tranquilizers?*

No, I am only able to provide biometric feedback. The doctor is currently under a lot of strain. I've been trying to lock the shuttle before he gets on board, but I believe someone is standing in the way.

Doug stopped moving. *You can hack the shuttle controls?*

Only the door features. I believe I must be in close proximity... Twerp continued speaking, but Doug had stopped listening, gaze riveted on the doctor's outstretched arms.

There was a way to keep Twerp out of Syndicorp's hands. It would be gruesome and allow the shuttle to escape, but there was no way Doug was reaching them in time with his legs offline. The doctor gained another two inches, solidifying Doug's decision. *Twerp, disable the door safety protocols and close them. Now!*

Twerp responded without question. The heavy sliding doors crunched through Dollard's forearms like a guillotine. Both appendages dropped to the deck in a spray of blood.

Attie tumbled backward, nearly falling on top of him.

The shuttle lifted into the air and pivoted, heading for the bulkhead opening. It passed through the atmospheric shield with a popping sound.

"Self-destruct in ten minutes. Final evacuation pods have been deployed to reach minimum distance from blast radius."

The siren stopped, leaving the bay in silence.

He stared at the glittering stars outside, dazed and reeling. Dollard was probably suffering a horrible death this very moment, but he found little satisfaction in the thought. It would be a sour victory if he didn't get Attie to safety, and she had little time to reach Rust at the shuttle. "Attie, get to the shuttle. Hurry!"

She had removed Twerp from Dollard's severed wrist, grimacing as she wiped the device off on the bottom of her pant leg. "All the shuttles are gone." Pocketing the AI, she moved to his side. "We have to find an escape pod."

His blood turned cold. Lifting his head, he gazed about the bay, confirming what she said. In his focus to reach Dollard, he hadn't realized the last shuttle had gone. The bay was empty of people jostling for shuttles. Emilryde still lay on his back several meters away, but he was the only cyborg in sight. Beyond that, the cavern was as quiet as a tomb. He muttered, "Should've known it would be too much to expect Rust to wait."

Attie helped him sit, eyeing his leg where the fabric just above his knee had been burned away along with most of the synth-skin beneath. "Do you think you can stand if I help you?" Her voice was surprisingly calm. "We need to get to the lift. There are no escape pods on this level."

"I'll only slow you down. Go without me. Hurry!"

Attie stared at him, realization settling over her features. "We're out of time to outrun the blast radius, aren't we?"

He shook his head, trying to stay positive for her. "You have to try. Run!"

Shaking her head, she sank to her knees beside him. "Can you try to stop the self-destruct?"

Her gorgeous blue eyes staring into his were breaking his heart. He touched her soft cheek, drawing back when he realized how filthy his hand was. "Even if I could get my nanites to work properly, we'd need the admiral's key. I failed you, Attie. I'm sorry."

"You did everything you could." Then Attie clutched his

arm, eyes widening. "Wait! The admiral's supposed to go down with the ship. We should go to the bridge!"

Doug smiled sadly. He loved her determination. "He was in on everything with Dollard. I doubt he was so honorable as to follow Syndicorp protocol and go down with the ship."

Tears glossed her eyes, and she dropped her chin. "You're probably right." She sighed and met his gaze once more. "Kiss me one last time?"

His chest swelled with love. In her final moments, she wanted his kiss. "You are the bravest, most tenacious woman I've ever met."

He leaned forward and met her lips, savoring their softness. Her rose petal scent washed over him, taking him back to the moments of pleasure they'd shared. She'd given him back his humanity, and although his time with her had not lasted nearly long enough, he was grateful.

The shush of the elevator doors carried across the quiet shuttle bay, interrupting his thoughts.

Rust stepped from the car and pelted toward them. Brix, Twobit, and Esben followed him.

"What the hell?" Doug asked. "You didn't take the shuttle? I thought you'd escaped without us!"

"Twobit discovered the admiral was still on board, so I went and got the self-destruct key." He brandished a flat, palm-sized card.

Twobit's face contorted with regret. "I thought I could hack into the self-destruct. But even with the card, I couldn't do it. There are too many firewalls."

"Of course there are," Doug snapped. "Self-destruct is supposed to be final."

"You're our best hacker," said Esben. "You need to try."

Rust tossed Doug the card. "If you don't, we're all dead. No pressure."

Doug caught it, clenching his hand tightly enough to bend the polymer. He was a bit surprised the admiral had stayed behind, but that was beside the point. "This can only be used on the bridge."

Offering a hand to help Doug to his feet, Rust said, "Get your ass to the bridge, then."

"Come on." Attie rose, tugging on his other arm. "There's still time."

Before he could try to stand, the cyborgs hoisted him into the air and rushed toward the lift. He could sense the minutes ticking down as they waited for the car to stop moving. Finally, the doors shushed open and the cyborgs deposited him in the admiral's chair on the bridge. The body of the admiral lay nearby, along with two other officers.

Smoke rose from several consoles, and the walls were blackened by weapons fire. The smell of melted polymer and hot metal filled the room as Doug shoved the card into a slot on the arm console. Closing his eyes, he reached for his nanites, trying to envision the self-destruct sequence. This would be the single-most important hack of his life.

And he had just over a minute to do it.

The admiral's chair gave him access to every aspect of the ship, and the colors and sounds clamoring for his attention were nearly debilitating. He struggled down one false trail after another. In a panic, he erected his own shielding to block irrelevant data, and continued on.

Then he saw it. A ticking clock, just ahead. *Thirty seconds and counting.*

A shimmering firewall surrounded the self-destruct sequence. The admiral's key had gotten him this far, but it wouldn't grant access through the firewall. He spiraled around it, looking for a chink in the armor. There was always a back door; programmers knew better than to build something they couldn't hack. But he couldn't find it.

Growing more frantic as the seconds ticked by, he slammed against the wall, brute force his last resort.

Then Twerp's voice reached him. *Over here, Doug.*

He spun, searching for the AI. He found her standing in a multicolored river of data, her ethereal form a willowy, feminine shape that shifted with the code's ebb and flow.

Sixteen seconds left.

She gestured to a spot high on the firewall. *I can't reach it.*

There it was; a single byte, so small he'd missed it.

An entry point.

Coiling all his energy, he narrowed his focus and leapt. He dropped his shielding, squeezed his virtual self until, with a pop, he slipped through.

On the other side was a simple timer with an on-off code right in the center. Eight seconds left. The clock was blinking, ticking them toward doom. Seven seconds. Six. Surely disarming it couldn't be this easy? Was it booby trapped?

Five seconds.

Booby trap or not, he was out of time. Holding his breath, he toggled it. Four seconds.

The clock blinked.

Four seconds.

Four seconds.

It had to blink three more times before his shoulders relaxed. *I did it*. Then he turned to Twerp, *We did it*!

He opened his eyes to the expectant faces around him. Attie gripped his human hand tightly, lips white with terror. Dirt smudged her cheek, and one shoulder of her tunic was torn. She was the most beautiful woman he'd ever seen.

"Well?" she asked.

In response, he grinned and pulled her onto his lap, capturing her mouth in a kiss.

From Attie's pocket, Twerp said, "The countdown has stopped. I estimate our odds of success were four billion, eight hundred and thirty-six thousand nine hundred to one, unless you take into account—"

Twobit shouted, "Holy fuck, he did it!"

The bridge erupted with cheers, covering the rest of Twerp's analysis. Rust and Brix high-fived each other with crashing force. Twobit pounded them on the backs.

Attie cupped Doug's face in both hands and returned his kiss, shaking with sobs and laughter.

He laughed with her. They were alive and they were together. He'd never been as happy as he was at this moment.

She lay her head against his chest and let out a slow breath. "I can't believe we survived."

"Survived?" Rust crowed, eyes gleaming. "We own a fucking flagship!"

As the truth settled in, Doug met the eyes of his crew with a grin. "Where do we want to go first?"

Chapter Twenty-Two

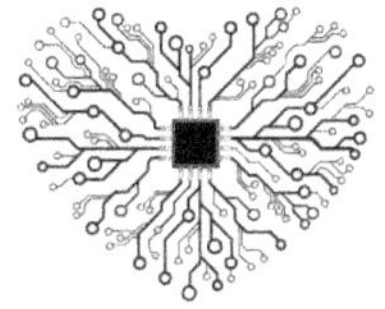

Attie rose from her seat at the bridge's comm, legs shaky as she stared at the star-filled view screen. The sound of the burn drive powering down to regular thrusters was music to her ears. They'd fled deep into unclassified space to throw off any pursuit. Syndicorp would undoubtedly try to get their flagship back, and even the *Icarus's* guns would be no match against a flotilla.

Now, after three hard burns in as many days, Attie just wanted a shower, a nap, and some food. The bridge was equipped with a massive nav-grav unit that didn't require people to be strapped in, but it didn't alleviate recovery time, and this many burns in such a short time left her feeling groggier than usual. Even the cyborgs seemed woozy, rubbing their heads and groaning.

"I think that should hide our trail," said Doug, swiveling in the admiral seat, cybernetic eye looking over the crew on the bridge.

Attie's gaze was drawn to his bare knees where the regrowing synth skin still looked patchy, mottled crimson over his polymer bones. Esben knew how to use a machine that accelerated cyborg healing, and even Emilryde and Benjy would be up and around in no time. It amazed her that they'd suffered no casualties.

"Twobit," Doug asked. "Think you can finish your sweep of the *Icarus* today?"

Instead of resting between burns like Attie, the cyborgs had been systematically going from room to room and eliminating any remaining signals Syndicorp might pick up on. Doug had his hands full figuring out the burn drive and navigation systems.

Rust stood and answered, "Aye, captain," while the other two nodded wearily.

Inhaling deeply, Attie headed to the door. "I'll go check the captives."

A handful of Syndicorp crew who'd been left behind— including a tech who'd been trapped in a cryopod—were in the brig until they could be dropped off somewhere.

Then there was Claudia. Attie had originally felt guilty for all but forgetting the other Consort during their mad dash to escape, but the woman had shrugged and told her she'd have done the same.

Claudia showed no desire to leave the Consort Chamber and only slipped out to get more drugs from the med kit in the security office. Attie was certain one of these times she'd find the woman dead of an overdose. *I need to ask if Esben has a way to break her addiction*, she reminded herself. If there was one thing she'd come to realize over the last few days, it was that you should never give up.

At the doorway, Doug put a hand on her arm, drawing her out of her thoughts. "When you've finished, come to the admiral's suite."

Butterflies filled her stomach. They hadn't been alone together since he'd hacked the countdown, but she'd caught him looking at her repeatedly between burns and hoped she knew what he was asking.

She yearned for him, too. The one time they'd been intimate invaded her mind every time she looked at him. But another part of her was terrified. The sex had been spectacular, but it had also been born of desperation and adrenaline. What if this time things fell flat?

There's only one way to find out, she told herself as she smiled and nodded at him.

A mix of exhaustion and anticipation made her insides jittery as she checked the brig, then hurried to her quarters to shower and change clothes. Her footsteps echoed hollowly in the vacant corridors. Hundreds of crew members had fled during the self-destruct sequence, and she could move to a nicer room if she wanted, but she hadn't taken time to think that far ahead. The cyborgs had moved out of their cells and into the officer suites two levels up.

Once she was clean and dressed, she headed to the lift. She stepped off the elevator on the officer level, and the mouthwatering scent of bacon hit her. She couldn't recall the last time she'd eaten anything but protein bars and electrolytes. Closing her eyes, she raised her chin and inhaled deeply, following the delectable smell down the hall.

At the admiral's suite, the door opened automatically, and the scent of the bacon grew stronger along with a delectable odor of fresh bread. Her stomach growled.

"I'm in here," Doug called from a doorway to her right.

Doug was cooking? And he could bake? She wasn't

certain why, but it surprised her. She stepped inside and let the door slide shut behind her.

She'd never been in the admiral's suite before and gaped at the open sitting area tastefully decorated with plush white furniture and glass shelving. This room alone was the size of the family quarters she'd grown up in. A vast video screen took up an entire wall, displaying an image of a spectacular orange sunset over rocky mountains capped with snow. She glanced toward another open door where she could see the corner of a large bed, dark blue coverlet falling in non-regulation fashion to the floor. Had he slept there, yet?

Heading into the dining area, she paused. Crystal glasses filled with orange juice sat at two adjacent spots on a big glass table, and a steaming pot of fresh coffee waited next to a fresh fruit platter.

This is for me. He could cook and he was thoughtful. Other guys she'd dated would've been waiting on the couch with a beer and thought themselves seductive if they remembered to offer her one, too. If she imagined she loved Doug before, she could practically worship him, now.

Carrying plates of bacon, eggs, and buttered toast, Doug emerged from a second door. He set the plates down and pulled out a chair for her. "I hope you don't mind breakfast. This is all I know how to cook."

Torn between jumping him now and her growling belly, she sat, letting him slide her forward. "Where did you get all this?" Reaching for a grape from the platter, she bit into it with a soft crunch that flooded her mouth with sweetness. "They only serve replicated food in the mess hall."

"The kitchen in the officer's mess has well-stocked coolers. I figured we might as well eat it before it goes bad." He reached for the coffee pot. "Coffee?"

"Nebulas, yes," she said, taking a huge bite of crisp bacon. She chewed with her eyes closed a moment, letting the rich, salty flavor fill her senses. When she opened her eyes, she found him looking at her, the coffee pot poised over the still-empty cup. She swallowed. "Aren't you going to eat?"

His gaze dropped to the mug, filling it and sliding it toward her. "It's been a long time since I shared a meal with someone. I like watching you enjoy it."

Heat flooded her, pooling low between her legs. She licked her lips, picked up a large grape and ran her tongue over it before biting in, eyes never leaving his. A slow moan of pleasure rose from her throat, but she wasn't really thinking about the food anymore.

Gaze smoldering, he slid his chair closer and put one hand on her knee. Electric jolts raced up her thigh. She'd worn slacks, but part of her wished she was wearing the thin consort skirt so he could slide the hem up and explore her further.

Putting one hand over his, she drew his touch along her leg to the juncture of her thighs.

He made a low, hungry sound at the back of his throat, and as if all he'd been waiting for was permission, he stood and pulled her into an embrace. His mouth claimed hers, kissing her with deep, passionate strokes of his tongue. Her hormones raged to life, and she melted against him, reveling in his taste and smell.

His desire prodded against her through the thin fabric of her slacks, and she slid one hand from his neck down his chest to loosen his drawstring waistband. Shoving his pants down his hips, her hands skimmed the perfect, rounded curve of his ass. He let the fabric slid to his ankles, stepping free before sweeping her into his arms.

Still kissing her, he carried her out of the dining area toward the bedroom. He lay her on top of the blankets, breaking away to pull his shirt over his head. His erection jutted from his hips as he grabbed her heels and pulled off her shoes simultaneously, tossing them to the floor behind him. Then he crawled up the bed to her waist. She was already fumbling at the clasp to her pants, but he finished the job, peeling them from her in a long sweep of his arm.

With both hands, he parted her thighs and nuzzled against her center. "I've been wanting to do this from the first moment I saw you naked on camera."

Flushing, she realized he'd probably watched her for a long time before ever meeting her in person. The cameras he'd hijacked likely looked right at her bed. *Nebulas, how many times did I use my vibrator while he was watching?*

She must've tensed, because he lifted his head to meet her eyes. "I tried not to watch you during personal moments. I just want you to know that. But I… couldn't look away."

Breath catching in her throat, she nodded at him. She probably would've watched him, too, if she'd had the chance. "It's okay."

He lowered his head again, breath hot against her sensitive flesh. "I know everything you like."

She shivered as he rolled his tongue over her clit, then dipped down around her lower lips and back up. He continued licking and sucking until she was pulsing and hot. Then his tongue plunged inside her, his face buried against her pussy.

Writhing, she clutched the back of his hair. Her other hand pinched her own nipple, bucking against him as he brought her higher and higher. But it wasn't enough. She needed more. "Doug—"

He inserted a long thick finger, and she rose over the crest, climaxing as he stroked and licked. He lapped up her juices like a man dying of thirst, until she slumped against the mattress, completely spent.

Leaving her throbbing pussy, he crawled up her body to claim her mouth, clasping the back of her neck with one hand. He kissed her with long, sure strokes of his tongue. The fingers of his other hand toyed with her nipple until it ached. Mouth still claimed, she clawed his back, wrapping her legs around his hips and drawing him against her until his shaft nudged her cleft, hot and solid.

"I want you inside me," she whimpered.

He chuckled, a deep, throaty sound that made her insides quiver. "You had only to ask."

Pulling back, he entered her in a sure, swift stroke that left her gasping. Her nipples hardened against his chest as he slid in and out, kissing her ravenously. He plunged forward so deep and hard, it almost hurt. But she wanted more, lifting her hips to meet his thrusts, aching for a second peak.

His hand released the back of her neck and he grabbed her hips, rolling to the side and lifting her so she straddled him. She liked being given control. Placing her hands against his chest, she arched her back, lifting almost free of his length before seating him fully inside her once more. Then she rolled her hips, rubbing his length along her inner ridges. The ecstasy of this moment, of their perfect rhythm together, made the world disappear.

She rode him up and up, until she seemed to leave her body and float in nothingness. The pressure inside her buoyed her beyond the stars. Doug roared, hands on her hips clamping her to him, hot seed filling her in pulsing gushes. Her second release seized her at the same time, consuming her, spiraling her in a shuddering wave of pleasure.

She fell forward against Doug's chest, breathing hard. She could hear his heartbeat beneath her ear. It might not be a human heart, but it was real. And it was hers.

He pushed a sweaty strand of hair from her cheek and kissed the top of her head. "I love you, Attie Swan. Thank you for rescuing me."

She sighed, heart full of love for him. "I love you, too, forever and always."

This man was hers. The future was hers.

Together, they could conquer anything.

Chapter Twenty-Three

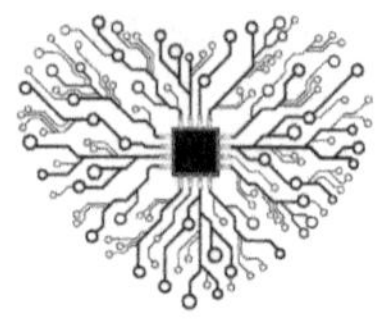

The *Hardship's* battered hull looked like something cobbled together by garan'uk children. As Doug watched it settle onto the *Icarus's* shuttle bay floor, he examined the mismatched plating and sensor arrays that didn't quite fit the space they'd been given. He didn't know a lot about ships, but this one had to be on its last legs.

Attie's hand squeezed his from where she waited beside him. "Excited?"

Doug nodded, trying to hide his worry. He hadn't spoken to his twin sister since helping her get rid of the nanites, and he hadn't seen her face to face much longer than that. What would she think of all his cybernetics?

"Stop worrying," said Attie, poking him in the side. "She's your sister. It's going to be okay."

The *Hardship's* cargo ramp popped open with a hiss and began descending with excruciating slowness, groaning as it moved.

Doug's impatience got the better of him. He strode forward and grabbed the lip, pulling until the base thudded against the deck.

A small figure threw herself against him in a full-body hug. "Doug! It's really you!"

"Hi, Lisa." He pressed his human cheek against her soft charcoal hair and lifted her in a bear hug. She'd always been much shorter than he was, but his cybernetic legs had given him another few centimeters of height. It felt good to be close to her again; being separated from her for so long had been like losing a limb—and he knew exactly how that felt.

Behind her, a blonde woman strode down the ramp, pistols jostling against each hip. She barely looked at them as she beelined it toward Attie. *Marlis.* He recognized her from the *Icarus's* security log. Two big Denaidan men with full beards lingered at the top of the ramp, pistols at their belts, eyeing him warily.

The other cyborgs had been worried about letting the pirates on board and were hanging back near the lift per Doug's instructions. He'd forbidden them to bring weapons today, but he wouldn't put it past Rust to have a pulse pistol or two stashed on his person just in case. Best to make introductions quickly so nothing went sideways.

He called, "Welcome on board the *Icarus*, Captain Qaiyaan."

Four Denaidans descended the ramp, copper skin reflecting the harsh lighting. Doug recognized the captain only from the many video feeds he'd hacked, but he knew Noatak in person from a brief encounter right here on the *Icarus*. Despite his better judgment, Doug had allowed this man's devotion to Attie's sister sway him and helped them both escape the ship, which had set in motion everything that had brought him to this moment.

He never would've guessed that one minor act of empathy would begin his own journey toward happiness.

Lisa released him with a little shove and looked up, her slate-gray eyes sparkling. "I can't believe you took over a

Syndicorp flagship! It's the only thing people are talking about in cartel space."

"It wasn't all me," he said, glancing toward his crew. Attie was a few feet behind him, hugging her sister. Tears glistened on her cheeks as the two of them rocked back and forth. "I want you to meet Attie and my crew."

Noatak stepped forward, eyes boring into Doug. "You're the cyborg who freed me." Without waiting for confirmation, he reached out and pulled Doug into a spine-cracking hug. "I owe you everything, *iluq*." He was as tall as Doug, and even without cybernetics, seemed to be just as strong. "Absolutely everything."

"Enough Noatak," Qaiyaan said. He gave Doug a sardonic smile. "My first mate isn't usually so demonstrative. But he's right, we are grateful for everything you've done."

"To be fair, I didn't do it for you." Doug looked at Lisa.

She smiled back as she slid an arm around Qaiyaan's waist. "Be nice, Doug. You two are brothers now."

Doug blinked, realizing just how true her words were. First, Doug became part of a cyborg brotherhood, then took a lover and befriended a sentient AI. Now he had a new sister and not one, but two brothers—Qaiyaan and

Noatak. His family seemed to get bigger every time he turned around.

Attie linked her arm through Doug's and leaned her cheek against his shoulder. "Marlis, this is Doug. Which one of these is yours?"

"My memory's still shit, but I'm pretty sure it's this one." Marlis hitched a thumb toward Noatak. "Noatak, this is my sister, Attie."

Noatak rolled his eyes and put one arm around Marlis's shoulders to jerk her close. "She's trouble, but she's all mine."

A rumbling sound made everyone turn as Twerp came off the lift, her treaded wheels loud against the decking. The boxy, meter-tall sweeper bot was the best the cyborgs had been able to manage for her, but Twerp was delighted to finally move around on her own. "Greetings!" Twerp's camera swiveled upward toward Marlis. "My facial recognition program is not yet complete, but I believe you must be Marlis. It is interesting to finally see you in person."

"Oh my God. It can't be—" Marlis's eyes went wide. "Twerp?"

Twerp's repurposed dust bin slid forward, revealing a tray with several glasses of pink liquid. "I have brought refreshments."

Attie let go of Doug's arm and picked up a glass. "I forgot to tell you, Marlis. Twerp survived."

Marlis blinked. "In a sweeper bot?"

"It is a long story," said Twerp, rolling forward a few inches and raising her dustbin of sloshing glasses. "I believe it is a human custom to regale each other with historical experiences over drinks. Emilryde assures me this is the same beverage served in the finest establishments on Enays. Please, try some."

Marlis shook her head and took a glass. "That's Twerp, all right. Never gets right to the point."

"*Ellam Cua*, Twerp!" A red-headed Denaidan with bare feet pushed forward, bending to look straight into the AI's camera. "You got your eyes!"

"Indeed I did." Twerp shuttered and opened her lens as if fluttering her lids. "I believe I recognize your voice from when you assisted me during Marlis's assimilation to the nanites. Are you Tovik?"

Tovik grinned and nodded. "Yep. Good to see you again, Twerp."

"I am most gratified to see you, as well. Would you care for a drink?"

"That'd be great." He picked up a glass and took a sip while he crouched down to examine Twerp's chassis. "Let me look at you. I've never seen a Syndicorp bot up close before."

"Twerp has the right idea." Attie pulled her sister toward several cargo containers the cyborgs had set up as tables laden with platters of food. "We put together a feast to celebrate. Come on."

Lisa grinned at Doug, then grabbed Qaiyaan's arm to drag him along. "I like her already."

It felt so good to be near Lisa again, and exponentially good that she and Attie were getting along. He hung back, watching everyone take seats and chat as if they'd known each other all along.

Rust took a seat next to Marlis, removing a pulse pistol from his boot and offering it to her, butt-first. *Damn that cyborg.* But Marlis pulled a pistol from her belt and offered it in return, obviously delighted to be talking guns.

Noatak leaned toward Doug. "Now we've lost her.

Marlis'll talk guns all night. Any chance there's a bottle of Kantarellian rum over there?"

Doug was surprised to realize he was grinning like an idiot. "I believe we can rustle up a bottle or two."

Attie called out, "Doug, you coming?"

He settled to the seat next to her. Attie touched the back of his hair with loving fingers, and when he looked at her, the love in her eyes made his cybernetic heart skip a beat. This woman had brought him everything he never thought he deserved. Everything he'd craved but been afraid to admit he wanted. She'd given him the most important thing in the universe. Her love had made him human again—had made him *whole* again. And he was going to spend the rest of his life proving he was worth it.

EPILOGUE

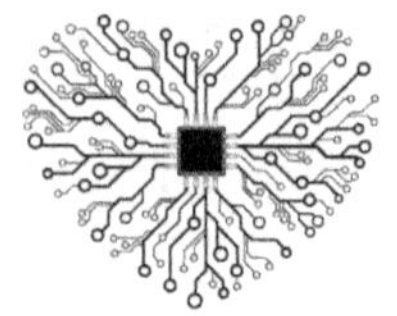

Father had been nearby; Rashana had felt his energy even through the deep sleep of her cryopod. *The cryopod he tricked me into.*

Extreme empathic and biometric sensitivity. That was her father's diagnosis. At the age of nine, she'd admitted to hearing voices. Then she got in an argument with her tutor, and he'd dropped dead right in front of her. Father said the death was her fault. That he would find a way to rein in her power. He wanted to use needles and tubes, and quarantined her to a lab until she was "fixed."

Mother said they should to train her not to do it again. Rashana wanted to cry when she thought of her mother's glorious blue skin and shimmering turquoise veins. For years, Mother had been her only view of the outside world. Her eyes and ears, her taste and touch. *Gone forever.*

Again, father blamed Rashana. Said she was a naughty girl, and her power was too strong. But Rashana didn't feel strong, waiting here in darkness, her anger never quite hot enough to free her from this never-ending stasis.

Father said he loved her. She heard the whispers of his mind every time he came within range of the cryopod. He said he was doing it for her own good. That he would find a way to keep her powers in check. To let her live a normal life.

Rashana didn't want a normal life. She wanted to punish him for making her angry. For tricking her. For stealing the very life he promised to give her.

If Rashana ever got free, she was going to burn his heart right out of his body.

Dear Reader,

Thank you for joining me for Doug and Attie's story. I hope you enjoyed their adventure as much as I did! The story continues in **Mated to Mek**, where our beloved doctor is about to have his bedside manner pushed to its limits.

Raised in a lab and experimented on by her own father, Rashana is a broken woman. But when she meets Mek, everything changes...

Get your copy of **Mated to Mek** now or keep reading for an excerpt!

XOXO

Tamsin

Mated to Mek
Excerpt

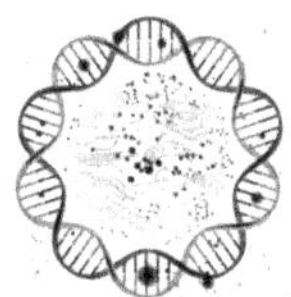

Mek stepped off the *Hardship's* ramp and into the cavernous flagship bay. Tools and supplies lay scattered across the deck, and a couple of charred spots on the deck were obviously from weapon fire. The *Icarus* was an incredible trophy for the rebellion; with its cyborg crew now joining their cause, the rebels might actually stand a chance against the evil corporation.

But right now Mek's mind wasn't on the rebellion. It was on the puzzling contents of a long metal cryo pod waiting at the far end of the deck.

Tovik, the *Hardship's* young engineer, thundered down the ramp behind Mek, his bare feet slapping the metal deck as he pelted toward the pod. Or, more likely, toward the blonde human female standing among the cyborgs grouped around it. Ever since the Denaidans had discovered nanites that would allow them to take human mates, Tovik was fixated on the opposite sex.

To be fair, most Denaidans were at the moment. After fifteen years without the ability to take mates, they had good reason. Mek, however, had little interest in pursuing a female. Any thoughts he had about sex tended to be clinical. He desperately needed to understand human physiology and support successful procreation between their species. So far, none of the pairings had successfully become pregnant, and without children, his race was still doomed. He didn't have time to dally with love.

Picking up his pace, he hurried toward the waiting group. Attie Swan was already mated to Doug, the *Icarus's* cyborg captain, and Tovik had a knack for saying the wrong thing at the wrong time. The last thing the rebellion needed was to alienate their new allies.

Thankfully, the kid seemed to be focused on the pod's glowing purple interface. His fingers tapped a rapid staccato against the pod's metal casing as he spoke. "...until the doc has a look."

A red-headed human cyborg took a half step forward as Mek drew near, fists clenched at his sides as if raring for a fight. "You're the doc, right?" he directed at Mek. "Let's bust it open."

Tovik vaulted over the pod to put himself between it and the cyborg. *"Uminaq,* no!" He shook his head violently. "Last time we found a cryo pod, there was a girl inside. Forcing it open might harm whoever's in there."

Attie nodded in support and shot a dirty look toward the cyborg who'd suggested breaking in. "That's why I insisted on having a doctor on hand before we do anything, Rust."

Doug tapped the pod's surface with a polymer fingertip. "The lid's locking mechanism uses a revolving algorithm that's impossible for even my skills to crack." His green cybernetic eye flashed. "Dollard went to great lengths to keep whoever or whatever's inside this thing secured."

"That asshole thought it was important enough to die for," said the Enayshuan cyborg, his metallic facial tattoos gleaming slashes against his dark skin. "He lost both arms trying to get it onto the shuttle."

"Hope the fucker took a long time bleeding out," muttered Rust.

"Well, you were wise to wait for me." Mek examined the glowing purple screen on the pod's dark metal surface. "This interface looks complicated." The biometric data was as confusing as the pod itself, with a mixture of information relevant to multiple species. Yet, the pod wasn't large enough to contain more than a single large cyborg. Wondering how big the occupant might be, he ran his fingertips over the lid. This pod wasn't a standard unit, and there wasn't even a window to view the occupant, which was a shame; knowing what sort of life form he'd be dealing with could help him prepare in the event things went sideways when it opened.

Straightening, he glanced toward where the *Hardship* sat parked on the deck of the shuttle bay, its mismatched plating and sensor arrays as unique to it as the cyborgs were to their implants. He had a decent stock of basic medical supplies on board, but the *Icarus* likely had a better facility.

"I assume you have a working med bay?" he asked. "I'd prefer to open this there in case something goes wrong."

"We were going to take it to Dollard's lab in case there's a cyborg inside, but one of the pod's mag lifts isn't working," said Doug, pointing to the head of the pod.

"And this damned crate's heavier than it has any right to be." Rust flexed both hands. "Either that, or my arms need recalibrated."

Tovik bent to examine the transportation clips at one end of the pod. "Bet I can fix that."

Knowing there was no holding the kid back when it came to mechanics, Mek sighed and nodded. "Fine. But don't touch the pod's controls, Tovik. The mag lift only."

"I promise," Tovik said, already prying open a control panel.

Leaving Attie to lend a hand finding parts, Doug led Mek to the lift and down several corridors into the flagship's belly until they reached the lab. Stainless steel exam tables had been pushed against the walls, and several cupboards hung open, exposing every type of medical equipment imaginable. There were signs of a fight here, too, with control panel wiring hanging from walls and a large stain on the floor that was most likely blood. Doors to what appeared to be prison cells stood open along three of the walls.

"This is the cybernetic lab," said Doug. "There's also a cloning lab, but someone turned off the incubators before the evacuation, and the place reeks. Or we have a standard med bay if you prefer."

Mek surveyed the tools and supplies scattered around the various lab tables. Compared to his tiny med bay on board the *Hardship,* this lab was a doctor's wet dream. The cupboards had everything from first aid supplies to more advanced tools he assumed were for cybernetic maintenance and repair. He grimaced when he noticed the thick, dangling straps on one exam table—it was very obvious the patients in this room hadn't always been willing.

"This should be fine." He began organizing equipment he thought he might need, including an emergency methane breather in case the pod held a species who couldn't breathe oxygen. Wondering how much longer Tovik would be, he glanced toward the nearest computer monitor. "Mind if I take a look at the doctor's research while I wait? I'm not too familiar with cyborg tech, and I might need it."

Doug nodded. "Have at it. We already hacked most of the firewalls."

Booting up a computer console, Mek skimmed several folders, uncertain about exactly where to start. Dollard had been cocky in assuming the flagship would success-fully self-destruct, or else he'd never have left so much information intact. There were hundreds of files detailing biological studies, cybernetic implants, and nanite inter-connectivity. Excitement swelled in Mek's chest. Information about the nanites might help with his current research.

The door whooshed open, and the pod came gliding into the room ahead of Tovik. "Told ya' I could get it working," the young engineer announced before pausing to ogle the lab equipment. He reached for a hunk of cable dangling from a many-armed contraption that looked uncomfortably like a torture device. "*Asirpaa!* What's this do?"

"Don't touch, kid," Doug said gruffly.

Tovik flushed and dropped his hand. "I was only curious."

Mek pulled a hard line from his computer and attached it to the pod's interface, hoping it might automatically bring up the proper files. A graph opened on the screen and he couldn't help smiling. *Finally, a stroke of luck.* He cycled through several data points before pausing on a biometric reading that appeared to be ionic.

He frowned. "This looks Denaidan."

Tovik pushed in to look over his shoulder. "One of us is in there? Really?"

"Only one way to find out." Taking a deep breath, Mek initiated the pod's waking cycle.

The pod gave a series of soft clicks, and with a whoosh, the chamber lid cracked down the middle, releasing a cloud of mist.

"*Uminaq!*" Mek's twin hearts thudded painfully against his ribs. A normal cryopod should take hours to establish equilibrium before it opened. Had he done something wrong? A rapid reawakening could cause severe cognitive damage or even death.

He waved one hand to clear the air, squinting through the thick clouds still billowing from inside. The lid had retracted into the base, but he couldn't get a clear view of the occupant. He stepped closer, leaning down for a look, and let out a sharp breath.

Reclining against an angled backrest rested not a cyborg or a Denaidan, but a female. A stunning, naked female.

Black hair with glinting silver highlights framed her high cheekbones and fanned over the swells of her bare breasts, while mist obscured her lower half. He'd never seen someone of his species with such pale, pearly skin, but she might have partial albinism. He longed to run his hands over every inch of her to see if she felt as silken as she appeared. To cup her breasts and taste the slight pout of her plump lower lip...

He shook his head, trying to clear it of wayward thoughts. It had been ages since he'd had this sort of reaction to a female, even a naked one.

Then her golden eyes opened, and he was sucked into a vortex of emotion.

Get your copy of **Mated to Mek** and keep reading now!

Glossary

- *Anaq* - Shit
- **Attahat wheel** - A form of gambling using a random wheel much like roulette
- **Burn** - The means by which ships travel long distances quickly using ionic frequencies to bend space
- **Cartel** - Organized crime ring
- **Cochlear implant** - A cybernetic device that transmits communications via vibrations directly against the bones of the ear
- **Cyborg** - A person with over 50% of their body replaced by cybernetic parts. Although many people have cybernetic enhancements, actual cyborgs are banned from Syndicorp citizenship.

- **Denaida-daru** - The Denaidan homeworld, destroyed by Syndicorp. Also called planet K-4H10
- *Ellam Cua* - The Denaidan deity
- **Enayshuan** - A human-like species with prominent eye ridges, known for their metallic body powder. Often associated with the sex trade
- **Enays** - A sex planet run by enayshuans
- **Finofan** - Aliens with iguana-like frills around their ears and slitted eyes. They like hot and humid atmosphere
- **Garan'uk** - A methane breathing alien species
- *Iluq* - Brother
- **Ionic power or shield** - A Denaidan ability to affect matter and gravity
- **Kwirn** - A form of gambling using 3-D tables and pieces
- **Nav-grav seats** - Used to keep humanoids comfortable during ship burn
- **Netorpok** - An exotic pet banned on most worlds
- **NIU** - Nanite Integration Unit, a clandestine Syndicorp lab with cyborg test subjects
- **Parsec** - A measurement of distance (3.2 light years)

- **Posungi** - An egg-laying alien with an orange tentacled face
- *Qumli* - Asshole
- **Rakwiji** - Scaled aliens with a poisonous claw, who hunt in pairs and require torture as part of their mating ritual. Often hired by the cartel as bounty hunters
- **Saluqan** - A race with an intuitive talent for medical skills. They have blue to purple skin and sometimes iridescent veins that show through the skin.
- **Sizantha pods** - Used to make tea
- **Syndicorp** - A mega-corporation that runs a huge section of the galaxy
- **Synth skin** - Artificially grown biological polymer that mimics actual skin. Most commonly used over cybernetic parts.
- **The Termination** - Syndicorp's destruction of Denaida-daru
- *Ucuk* - Dick
- *Uminaq* - Dammit
- **Unclassified space** - Areas of the galaxy not ruled by Syndicorp
- **Xeimir worm** - A glossy-skinned alien that breathes through its skin and is ultra-sensitive to light

- **Yanipa-nimayu** - A six-legged alien often found performing manual labor

Sexy shifter heroes and fierce heroines in the wilds of Alaska.

About the Author

Once upon a time I thought I wanted to be a biomedical engineer, but experimenting on lab rats doesn't always lead to happy endings. Instead, I turned my nerdy fascination with science into stories filled with alien pirates, monsters, and character-driven romance with guaranteed happily-ever-afters.

My books feature feisty heroines, tortured heroes, and just enough science fiction or magic to get them into all kinds of steamy trouble. My monsters always find their mates—and I promise my stories will never leave you hanging (although you may still crave more).

When I'm not writing, you'll probably find me in the garden or the kitchen, exploring Alaska with my husband, or preparing for the zombie apocalypse. I also enjoy crocheting while binge-watching Netflix, playing video games, and spending family time during our weekly D&D sessions.

Want more stories from my worlds?

Join my VIP Club to receive free books, bonus scenes, sneak peeks, and exclusive updates.

https://www.tamsinley.com/join-club

bookbub.com/authors/tamsin-ley

goodreads.com/TamsinLey

facebook.com/TamsinLey

amazon.com/author/tamsin